"We have business to discuss."

"What sort of business?"

"You've suffered an injustice at Venstar. If that was—indirectly—my fault, I can only apologize," Andreo murmured dryly. "In the short term it makes more sense for me to find a better position for you in another company."

Pippa had grown very tense. "I don't need your help…."

Andreo expelled his breath out on an impatient hiss. "I'm not offering help. I'm trying to redress a wrong. There's a subtle distinction."

An uneasy flush had lit her cheekbones. "What's done is done…. I can look after myself. Don't you think that I can manage on my own? You're not responsible for me—"

"Maybe I *feel* responsible? But naturally I'll respect your wishes."

"Will you really? Even though you think my wishes are rubbish and you really hate people disagreeing with you? Will I have to grovel to get back in with you again?"

Andreo's appreciative gaze narrowed to a blazing sliver of raw gold. "Just share my bed, *amore*."

BRIDES OF L'AMOUR

*The mother, the mistress
and the forgotten wife*

Tabby, Pippa, Hilary and Jenny: four friends
whose lives were changed forever in their teens
by a tragic accident. But the wheel of fortune
must turn up as well as down, and these
young women are about to get their share of
blessings…in the shape of three gorgeous men.
Christien, Andreo and Roel
are all determined to woo them
and wed them…whatever that takes!

Brides of L'Amour:

November 2003: **The Frenchman's Love-Child**
Tabby and Christien's story #2355

January 2004: **The Italian Boss's Mistress**
Pippa and Andreo's story #2367

March 2004: **The Banker's Convenient Wife**
Hilary and Roel's story #2379

Lynne Graham

THE ITALIAN BOSS'S MISTRESS

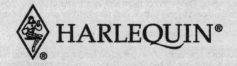

TORONTO • NEW YORK • LONDON
AMSTERDAM • PARIS • SYDNEY • HAMBURG
STOCKHOLM • ATHENS • TOKYO • MILAN • MADRID
PRAGUE • WARSAW • BUDAPEST • AUCKLAND

ISBN 0-373-12367-1

THE ITALIAN BOSS'S MISTRESS

First North American Publication 2004.

Copyright © 2003 by Lynne Graham.

This edition published by arrangement with Harlequin Books S.A.

Visit us at www.eHarlequin.com

Printed in U.S.A.

CHAPTER ONE

A TEAM had flown over to Naples to bring Andreo up to speed on his latest acquisition, Venstar.

Tensions were running high for there was not a single Venstar executive present who did not feel that his job might be on the line. The ruthlessness that distinguished Andreo D'Alessio's brilliance in the business world was a living legend.

'This should help you to fit faces to the senior staff when you come over to visit us,' one of the directors said with a rather nervous laugh as he passed over a company newsletter adorned with a photograph of key personnel.

Andreo D'Alessio studied the front page with keen dark eyes. Only one woman featured in the line-up and he only noticed her in the first instance because she messed up the picture. She was very tall and her stooped and self-effacing stance shrieked all the awkwardness of a very skinny baby giraffe striving in vain to hide its overly long limbs. Heavy framed spectacles dwarfed her thin, earnest face. But what had caught Andreo's attention was her pronounced untidiness. Stray riotous curls stuck out from her head hinting that her hair was in dire need of a good brushing. His frown deepening, he went on to note that her ill-fitting suit jacket was missing a button and the hem on one leg of her shapeless trousers was sagging. He almost shuddered. The epitome of cool elegance himself, he was less than tolerant of those who offended his high standards.

'Who is the woman?' he enquired.

'*Woman?*' Andreo was asked blankly and he had to point her out in the photograph before his companions made the necessary leap in understanding.

'Oh, you mean…*Pippa!*' a Venstar executive finally exclaimed as though challenged to recognise the reality that the senior staff actually harboured a female in their ranks. 'Pippa's our assistant finance manager—'

'You don't tend to think of her as being a woman…has a brain like a calculator. An academic high-flyer who thinks of nothing but work,' a director proclaimed with appreciation. 'She's absolutely dedicated. She hasn't taken a single holiday in three years—'

'That's unhealthy,' Andreo cut in with disapproval. 'Stressed and exhausted employees operate below par and make mistakes. The lady needs a vacation and HR should have a word with her about smartening up her slovenly appearance.'

Jaws dropped. Paunches were sucked in and jackets smoothed down for none of the men was quite sure which imperfections might put one at risk of attracting the clearly very dangerous label of being 'slovenly'. An uncomfortable silence fell. Slovenly? *Was* Pippa slovenly? Nobody had ever really looked at Pippa long enough to have noticed one way or the other. That she was an economics prodigy and very efficient was all anybody had ever cared about.

Still scanning the picture to note the level of personal care as displayed by the male contingent of the line-up, Andreo found yet more scope for censure. 'I don't believe in the concept of dressing down because it doesn't impress clients. I don't want to see jeans in the office. A smart appearance implies discipline and it *does* impress. This man here could do with a haircut and a new shirt.'

He pointed out the offender in an impatient tone. 'Attention to self-presentation is never wasted.'

Almost every man in the room decided to go on a diet, get a haircut and buy a new suit. Andreo, all six feet five inches of him, after all, could be seen to practise what he preached. Lean, mean and undeniably magnificent in a to-die-for Armani designer suit, Andreo was an impressive enough sight to inspire the younger men with an eager desire to emulate him. Ricky Brownlow, however, who was far too vain of his blond good looks to believe himself in need of either a diet or a haircut, concealed a self-satisfied smile. He had just worked out how he could promote his current lover over Pippa's head without attracting undue criticism.

'The HR department also needs to set new targets. I want to see a *very* rapid improvement in Venstar's abysmal record of promoting women to executive level,' Andreo concluded.

When her immediate superior, Ricky Brownlow, invited her into his office and broke the bad news, Pippa was betrayed into a startled exclamation. 'Cheryl…is going to be the new finance manager?'

Ricky nodded in casual confirmation as if there were nothing strange about that development.

Cheryl Long? The giggly brunette who currently acted as her junior was now to become her *boss?* That bombshell sent Pippa into severe shock. After all, she herself had been Acting Finance Manager for almost three months and she had had high hopes of the position being made permanent. Until that moment she had had no idea that Cheryl had even applied for the job.

'I thought that I should let you know before HR informed you through official channels,' Ricky added in the tone of a man who had gone out of his way to do her a favour.

'But Cheryl has hardly any qualifications and only a couple of months of experience in the section...' Pippa was quite unable to conceal her astonishment.

'New blood keeps the company fresh and sharp.' Ricky Brownlow frowned at her in reproof and a painful flush lit her fair skin.

A slender young woman with shaken blue eyes and vibrant auburn curls scraped back from her brow and held tight by a clip, Pippa walked back to her desk. She *could* have taken losing out to a superior candidate, she told herself urgently. But was she just being a bad loser? Shame at the fear that she might be that petty consumed Pippa, who suffered from a conscience more over-developed than most. Self-evidently, she decided, Cheryl Long had talents that she herself had failed to recognise.

The animated buzz of dialogue around Pippa reminded her of the party being held that evening to welcome Andreo D'Alessio and she suppressed an exasperated sigh. She had never liked parties and she liked work so-cial occasions even less. However, now that she had been turned down for the job that she had naively assumed was in the bag, she had better make an appearance at the celebrations lest other people start thinking that she be-grudged Cheryl her good fortune.

Cheryl was about to become her boss. Pippa swal-lowed the thickness building in her tight throat. For good-ness' sake, had she screwed up somewhere so badly that she had blown her own promotion prospects right out of the water? If that was the case, why hadn't she been told and at least warned of her mistake? Cheryl was going to be her boss. Cheryl, whom Pippa had had to be rather stiff with on several recent occasions for her incredibly long lunch breaks and shoddy work? Cheryl, who seemed to spend half the day chatting and the rest of it flirting with the nearest available male? Cheryl, who was mercifully on leave that day...

Pippa sank deeper and deeper into shock. Hothoused as she had been from preschool level right through to university, and always expected to deliver exceptional results, failure of any kind threw her into an agony of self-blame and self-examination. Somehow, somewhere, she was convinced, she had fallen seriously short of what was expected of her...

'I wish he was more into publicity and we had a better photograph of him,' one of the project assistants, Jonelle, sighed in a die away voice that set Pippa's teeth on edge. 'But we'll see if he lives up to his extraordinary reputation when we see him in the flesh tonight—'

Her companion giggled. 'He's supposed to have bought his last girlfriend a set of diamond-studded handcuffs...'

Pippa had no need to ask who was under discussion for Andreo D'Alessio's exploits as an international playboy, business whizkid and womaniser were very well documented for a male who went to great lengths not to be photographed. Her soft full mouth curled in helpless disgust. The man that offered *her* diamond-studded handcuffs as a gift would find himself skydiving without a parachute. But then no man was ever likely to offer her diamond-studded sex toys of any description, and very grateful she was too not to be the type to attract that kind of perverted treatment! Just listening to another female agonise in fascination over a male set on reducing her sex to the level of toys for fun moments made her feel ill.

'I bet he's an absolute babe.' Jonelle had a dreamy look on her pretty face. 'Hot stuff—'

'I bet he's small and rather round in profile just like his late father,' Pippa inserted with deliberate irony. 'And the reason that Andreo D'Alessio doesn't like publicity is that he loves the rumour that he's much bigger and better looking than he really is.'

'Maybe the poor guy is just sick of being chased for his mega-millions,' Jonelle opined in reproach.

'And maybe he wouldn't be chased at all if he didn't have them,' Pippa mocked.

Mid-morning she was called to an HR interview. Informed for the second time that her application to become Finance Manager had been unsuccessful, she felt grateful but still a little surprised that Ricky Brownlow had been kind enough to forewarn her of the disappointment coming her way. When she asked if there had been any complaints about her work performance, the older man was quick to reassure her.

'And that's very much to your credit when one considers events in recent months,' the HR director continued in a sympathetic tone.

Picking up on that oblique reference to her father's death in the spring, Pippa paled. 'I've been lucky to have my work to keep me busy.'

'Are you aware that you haven't utilised your holiday entitlement in several years?'

Her fine brows pleated and she shrugged. 'Yes…'

'I've been asked to ensure that you take at least three weeks off effective from the end of this month—'

'Three weeks…*off?*' Pippa gasped in dismay.

'I've also been authorised to offer you the opportunity of a sabbatical for six or twelve months.'

'A...a sabbatical...are you serious?' Pippa exclaimed in an even greater state of disconcertion.

Impervious to Pippa's discouraging response, the older man went on to wax lyrical about the benefits of taking a work break. He pointed out that Pippa had not taken a gap year between school and university and had in fact commenced employment at Venstar within days of her graduation.

'You spend very long hours in the office.'

'But I *like* working long hours—'

'Nevertheless I'm sure that you will enjoy de-stressing during your holiday in two weeks' time and that you'll consider the opportunity of extending your break with a sabbatical. Think of how refreshed you would be on your return to work.'

De-stressing? Ultra sensitive, Pippa picked up on that word and wondered if that was why she had been passed over in the promotion stakes. Did she come across as stressed to her colleagues? Irritable? Or was it that she seemed lacking in management skills? There had to be a reason why she had been unsuccessful—there *had* to be! Whatever, she was not being given a choice about whether or not she took a holiday and that bothered her. Why now and not before? Was there concern that she might not adapt well to the new command structure in the finance section?

Deeply troubled by her complete loss of faith in her own abilities, Pippa worked through her lunch hour and when, around three that afternoon, she glanced up and saw the empty desks around her, she frowned in surprise.

'Where is everybody?' she asked Ricky Brownlow when she saw him in his office doorway.

'Left early to get ready for the party. You should be heading home too.'

Pippa hated to leave a task unfinished but then she recalled the events of the day and the holiday that had been pressed on her. That had been a hurtful lesson in the reality that she was not indispensable. Rising from her desk, she lifted her bag. She had reached the ground floor before she appreciated that the rain was bouncing off the pavements outside and, in her haste to depart, she had left her coat behind.

Too impatient to wait on the lift again, she took the stairs. The finance floor was silent and she was walking towards the closet where her coat hung when she heard Ricky Brownlow's voice carrying out from his office.

'When I was in Naples, Andreo D'Alessio made it very clear that he likes sexy, fanciable women around him,' Ricky was saying in a pained, defensive tone. 'He took one horrified look at the piccy of our Pippa Plain in the company newsletter and it was clear that she would never fit the executive bill in his eyes, so I backed Cheryl's application instead. Cheryl's less qualified, I grant you, but she's also considerably more presentable—'

Pippa had frozen in her tracks. Pippa…*Pippa Plain*?

'Pippa Stevenson is an excellent employee,' a voice that she recognised as belonging to one of the older directors countered coldly.

'She's an asset as a backroom girl but her best friend couldn't call her a looker *or* a mover or shaker. She has all the personality of a wet blanket,' Ricky Brownlow pronounced with a viciousness that flayed Pippa to the bone. 'To be frank, I didn't think we'd be doing ourselves any favours if we ignored D'Alessio's sexist preferences and served up Pippa Plain to him on his first day here!'

Shattered by what she had overheard but even more terrified of being found eavesdropping, Pippa crept back out to the corridor and fled without her coat. In that one devastating dialogue, she had learned why Cheryl instead of herself was to be Venstar's next finance manager. *Pippa Plain?* Her tummy rolled with nausea but she refused to let herself cringe. Ricky Brownlow had laid it on the line: unlike Pippa, Cheryl was extremely attractive and popular with men. The curvaceous brunette's looks rather than her ability had influenced her selection.

A cold, sick knot of humiliation in her stomach, Pippa swallowed hard and blinked back stinging tears. It was so unfair. That job had had her name on it and she had worked darned hard for promotion. Nobody had the right to judge another person on their appearance. It was utterly wrong and against all employment legislation and Venstar deserved to be sued for treating her so shabbily. She imagined standing up at a tribunal and being forced to relate Ricky's demeaning comments and compressed her lips with a shudder of recoil. No, there was no way that she would take the company to a tribunal and make herself an object of sniggering pity.

Her best friend couldn't call her a looker...Pippa Plain? Was that a fact? Doubtless Ricky would never credit that when she was fifteen years old a modelling agency had offered her a lucrative contract. Of course, her father had been outraged by the mere suggestion that his daughter would engage in what he deemed to be a lowbrow career. But for the eight years that had followed Pippa had secretly cherished the memory of her one stolen day of rebellion against Martin Stevenson's strict dictates. She had gone to the agency in secret and let them make her up and do her hair. She had watched in fascination as cosmetic magic and clever clothing had transformed her from a pale, skinny beanpole into a glowing, leggy beauty. Then the old lech of a photographer had made a pass at her and sent her fleeing for home again,

convinced that everything her father had said about the
dangerous corruption of the modelling industry was true.

Why shouldn't she try to effect even some small part
of that transformation on her own behalf? She could at-
tend the party looking her best just to confound Ricky
Brownlow and that sexist louse, Andreo D'Alessio. How
could a man be so stupid that he put beauty ahead of
brains even in a business capacity?

Standing in the rain getting absolutely soaked through,
Pippa dug out her mobile phone and rang her friend
Hilary. Hilary Ross was a hairdresser and when asked if
she could squeeze Pippa in for a last-minute hair-rescue
mission, she was so taken aback by the request that she
gasped, 'Are you being frivolous at last? Is it Christmas
or something?'

'Or something,' Pippa confirmed a little unevenly. 'I'm
going out tonight and it's really important.'

Hilary had a heart the size of a world globe and told
her to come straight over, while adding that Pippa should
have known better than to think that she had to phone
and ask one of her oldest friends for an appointment.
'Especially when you only make the effort to get your
hair done about once a year!' she teased in conclusion.

Pippa caught an underground train that would take her
to Hilary's salon in the west London suburb of
Hounslow. As she was jostled by other passengers while
she stood in the aisle because there were no seats available Pippa's teeming thoughts were troubled. Sad though
it was to acknowledge, she was relieved that her father
was not alive to be shamed and disappointed by her failure to win promotion. But then when had she ever managed to meet her parent's expectations and make him
proud of her? she asked herself with pained and guilty
regret.

Her mind travelled back almost six years to the summer that her family life had been destroyed. She had been just seventeen when her parents and three other families had gone on their final holiday together to the Dordogne region of France. Her friendship with Hilary Ross stretched back as far as their childhoods. The Ross family had been part of the group that had gone to France and as the holiday had been an annual event there had been no reason to suspect that that year would be any different from any previous year. But that particular summer everything that could have gone wrong *had* gone wrong. In fact it had been a disastrous vacation for all concerned but nobody had had the nerve to admit that and it had still lasted almost the full six weeks.

No sooner had they arrived in France than her then best friend, Tabby, had got involved in a passionate secret fling with a French guy staying nearby and had become so besotted that she had scarcely noticed that Pippa had been alive for the remainder of their stay. During that same period, however, Pippa had had her heart broken and her self-esteem smashed without anybody even noticing.

But the conclusive life-altering event of that fatal holiday had been the dreadful car accident that had left Pippa's mother dead and put her father into a wheelchair. Tabby's father, Gerry Burnside, had got drunk and crashed a car full of passengers, shattering the lives of all his friends. Pippa had been much closer to her mother than she had ever been to her harsh and demanding father and she had been devastated by her mother's sudden death. Before the crash her father had been a science teacher and an active sportsman and he had never managed to come to terms with his disability.

Furthermore, as a young man Martin Stevenson had

wanted to be a doctor but had narrowly missed out on the exam grades required. From the hour of Pippa's birth, her father had been determined that his daughter should live out his dream of becoming a doctor for him and she had been pressed into doing her academic best from a very early age. But the consequences of that appalling car accident, which had also claimed the lives of Tabby's father, Hilary's parents and both Jen's and Pippa's mothers had traumatised Pippa and she had had to tell her father that she could not face a career in medicine.

The cruel intensity of her father's disappointment had been almost more than Pippa's conscience could bear and his bitterness had been terrible to live with. For nearly six years afterwards, Pippa had nonetheless been her parent's main carer. But, no matter how hard she had worked to please him with high grades in the economics degree she'd pursued and with tender care of his needs at home, he had never forgiven her for turning her back on the chance to become a doctor. Pippa remained wretchedly aware of what she saw as her own shortcomings. She was totally convinced that the really gutsy woman whom she wanted to be would have been fired by an unquenchable desire to study medicine after that car accident rather than put off for life and convinced that she was too soft to last the course.

When she made herself remember just how much she had once adored France, she could hardly credit that she had not visited the country of her own mother's birth since that tragic summer. She had even made excuses to avoid attending Tabby's wedding. Thankfully, however, Tabby's husband, Christien, brought his wife over to London on regular visits, so Pippa had been able to maintain contact with her friend. But wasn't it really past time that she came to terms with her mother's death and visited Tabby and Christien at Duvernay, the Laroche family's beautiful château in Brittany? How often had her friend invited her? Her conscience twanged. Shouldn't she spend at least part of the holiday she had to take with Tabby in France?

'Oh, no, this is the day you close at lunchtime and I completely forgot!' Pippa groaned in dismay when Hilary, having met her at the door of her tiny apartment took her across the passage into the hairdressing salon, which was strikingly silent and empty. 'For goodness' sake, why didn't you remind me that it was your half-day?'

Hilary was small and slim with enormous grey eyes and spiky blonde hair that had the very slightest hint of blue to match her T-shirt. Only a year Pippa's junior, she actually looked barely eighteen and she grinned. 'Are you kidding? Do I look that patient? You're finally going out on a date and I can't wait to find out who the bloke is!'

Pippa stiffened. 'There's no bloke. It's the big party for the new MD tonight—'

'But you were all out of breath on the phone and I thought you were excited—'

'Not excited…upset,' Pippa conceded jerkily. 'I bombed out at work, I fell *flat* on my face—'

'What on earth—?'

'I didn't get the job,' Pippa muttered in a wobbly undertone and then the whole unhappy story came tumbling out.

Hilary listened and tried not to wince while she dug into a cupboard in the tiny staff room and poured Pippa a stiff drink from the brandy someone had given her at Christmas.

'I don't touch it, you know I don't…' Pippa attempted to push the glass away.

'You're as white as a sheet. You need a boost.' Hilary pressed her down into a seat by the washbasins and deemed a change of subject the best policy. 'So you want to knock 'em dead in the aisles at Venstar tonight—'

'Some chance!' Wrinkling her nose at the taste, Pippa drank deep and the unfamiliar alcohol ran like fire down into her cold, empty tummy. Like the warmth of her friend's sympathy, however, it was a soothing sensation and she was incredibly grateful that she had ignored her father's withering sarcasm and had attended her first school reunion just a few months earlier. After Tabby had made a permanent move to France, Pippa had been delighted to meet up with Hilary again at the reunion and learn that the blonde also lived in London. After that tragic car accident, their paths had been forced apart and Tabby and Pippa had lost touch with Hilary and with the fourth member of that teenage friendship, Jen Tarbert.

'Even blindfolded, you could knock 'em dead,' Hilary repeated with determination, trying not to think unkind thoughts about Pippa's deceased father. However, it was an unfortunate truth that even when Pippa had been a child her parent had been a domineering bully with a wounding tongue and he had done a real hatchet job on his daughter's self-esteem.

While Hilary washed her hair, Pippa remembered to ask after her friend's kid sister, Emma. 'How's she doing?'

Hilary chattered on happily about the teenage sister she adored before saying, 'Will you let me do your make-up too?'

'If you don't mind...'

'Why would I mind? I *love* doing faces!'

'Well, you can only do your best—'

'With a bone structure as good as yours, I would hope

so.' Hilary watched Pippa stiffen and sighed before she pressed another brimming glass of brandy into the red-head's hand, told her that she was far too tense and hustled her upstairs to her cluttered apartment.

'I'll have to rush home to get changed,' Pippa remarked.

'You haven't got the time. You'll be late enough as it is.' Hilary hurried into her sister's bedroom and plundered the packed wardrobe there to emerge with a strappy dress in a glorious shade of turquoise.

'I can't borrow anything that belongs to your sister!' Pippa protested.

'Emma decided that this made her look too old and you know how picky teenagers are...there's no way she'll ever wear it now.'

'I wouldn't feel comfortable in a style like that,' Pippa muttered.

'Lighten up, Pippa,' Hilary urged in a pained tone. 'You're young and you can wear just about anything with your figure. It's not a revealing dress, so what are you worried about?'

In Pippa's opinion any garment that bared her shoulders, her thin arms and the sheer pitiful tininess of her breasts *was* much too revealing. Yet, her friend was being so kind and supportive that she was reluctant to reject her generosity. Both women wore the same size in shoes but, yet again, there was a great gap between their personal preferences. Hilary adored shoes with high heels whereas Pippa rarely wore heels because she already stood five feet eleven inches in her bare feet. A pair of three-inch high gold beaded sandals were set beside the dress and then Hilary showed her guest into the bathroom to enable her to take a shower before her transformation commenced.

Almost two hours later, and only after Pippa had donned the contact lenses she carried in her bag but rarely utilised, Hilary whisked the towel off the mirror and marched Pippa in front of it. 'You look totally, incredibly gorgeous and if you argue about that I swear I'm going to have a fight with you!'

In shocked silence, Pippa stared at her colourful reflection. 'I don't look like me—'

'No offence intended, but that's only because "me" neglects her hair, never wears make-up and can't be bothered dressing up!'

Pippa's eyes stung a little but she could hardly blink for the amount of mascara on her lashes. She swallowed hard and said gruffly, 'Thanks. I don't look like a loser and you wouldn't believe how much that means to me.'

Andreo D'Alessio was bored. He was also in a very bad mood.

He had not asked for a party. He had not wanted a party. He disliked surprises and he did not think that surprise parties had a role to play in the business world. He was not entertained by long speeches either. He had even less time for flattery and employees in a high state of excitement, particularly when it was obvious that a healthy proportion had overindulged in alcohol before attending the event. Having left the conference hall with the excuse of an important call, he was crossing the hotel foyer when he saw the ravishing redhead. Then he saw her, so stunning that she stopped him in his tracks.

Hair the rich colour of heavy cinnamon silk tumbled to her shoulders in a smooth, shining fall that reflected the light and framed an oval face of perfect symmetry. Her eyes were the clear, bright blue of the midsummer sky, her full mouth painted coral-pink to highlight the invitation of her soft lips. Her height alone would have attracted his attention for she was unusually tall for a woman. Nearly six feet in height, Andreo calculated with appreciation, and still confident enough to wear high heels. Of all things he abhorred the absurdity of trying to match his own very tall, well-built frame to that of some tiny, birdlike creature half his size. The redhead with her taut white shoulders, slender feminine curves and wondrously endless and shapely legs would *fit* him to perfection...

That fast, voracious male hormones kicking into lusty overdrive at the enervating prospect of the precise intimate fit of the gorgeous woman he was watching, Andreo decided that he was surveying his next lover.

Pippa gazed into the crowded conference hall, which was buzzing with Venstar employees, and wondered if anyone would even recognise her. With the curls she loathed straightened by Hilary's expertise with a blow-dryer, her spectacles discarded and in borrowed finery, she looked different. The amount of male attention she had attracted since her arrival at the vast hotel had made her very aware of that fact.

Unfortunately, the girlie dress made her feel horribly exposed and self-conscious. She wasn't used to men staring at her and all her life she had been shy. Got up in a no-nonsense trouser suit with work-related issues providing the framework for every dialogue with male colleagues, she had managed fine. But, shorn of that sensible façade, it was a challenge to appear impervious to the lustful appraisals she was receiving. Her chin tilting, she was on the brink of entering the hall when sudden silence fell within. Seeing the man moving towards the podium on the platform, she decided to stay where she was until he had finished making his speech.

As the speaker took up position Pippa stared and then laughed out loud. Oh, dear, Jonelle and every other woman fantasising about the physical attractions of the billionaire Andreo D'Alessio were suffering a very big let-down indeed to their wild fantasies.

'Care to share the joke?' a male voice urged lazily by her side.

Pippa stiffened in surprise for she had not noticed that there was a man standing that close and she felt far too awkward to turn her head to look at him direct. 'I was just thinking that a lot of people must have been very disappointed with Andreo D'Alessio,' she said a little breathlessly.

Disconcerted, Andreo frowned. 'And why would you think that?'

Something in that accented drawl sent a tiny little shiver of warning down her spine and might have silenced her had not Pippa been in the mood to be sharp, rather than soothing. 'I suppose that I should've said that the women will be disappointed. He's not even a little bit fanciable,' Pippa remarked with some satisfaction.

'No?' At that point, Andreo believed that she was only pretending not to know who he was. After all, the Venstar shindig had kicked off over an hour earlier and he had been the centre of attention from the outset. He assumed she was making a move on him and, having been subjected to some strange pick-up routines in his time, he was curious to see where she planned to travel after such an opening.

'No, he's downright short. In fact, he's so small, he would look more at home sitting under a mushroom dressed all in green like a leprechaun,' Pippa pronounced.

Belatedly, Andreo realised that she was studying Salvatore Rissone, whom he planned to put in charge of

Venstar after the business had been restructured. 'Height is not everything.'

'He looks like he's rather too fond of his food as well,' Pippa added with a cruelty that was quite unlike her. 'And he's definitely going bald. No wonder he doesn't like publicity photos. He's not exactly Mr Universe, is he?'

'Movie-star looks are not required in business.' Andreo was angered by her unkind comments about Sal's homely appearance. 'He is a fine man—'

'No, he's *not*,' Pippa cut in with growing heat. 'Andreo D'Alessio is a very rich man and the only reason people talk him up is because they're either hugely impressed by his money or...' As she spun round, giving way to her hurt resentment of Andreo D'Alessio to address her companion direct, she looked at him for the first time and what she was about to say went clean out of her mind again.

It was rare for Pippa to be forced to look up at a man. But what sent her brain into free fall was the sheer dazzling effect of this particular male animal up close. From the bronzed skin enhancing the lean, hard, elegant planes of his proud cheekbones to the stubborn masculine angularity of his jawbone, he was strikingly handsome. His mouth was wide and firm, his brows level and dark to match the gleaming luxuriance of his cropped black hair. But it was the piercing quality of eyes dark as ebony and accentuated by a frame of lush inky lashes that entrapped her.

'*Or...?*' Andreo collided with her turquoise gaze and found his annoyance mysteriously evaporating beneath the onslaught of those spectacular eyes. She was staring up at him in the most uncool way, her response to his sexual magnetism patent in her dilated pupils, and amused satisfaction gripped him.

She really *didn't* know who he was. She really had mistaken Sal Rissone for him. She was not teasing him or trying to capture his interest with a novel approach. Perhaps he was at risk of turning into one of those painful guys who took himself much too seriously, Andreo reflected abruptly. He decided that he ought to be challenged rather than antagonised by the unusual experience of hearing himself criticised. It certainly made a change from the fawning flattery that had been his lot throughout the evening.

'Or...?' Pippa was magnetised by his proximity and inexplicably feeling very short of breath.

'You were saying that people talk up Andreo D'Alessio because he is wealthy and *because*...?'

'His reputation scares them half to death,' Pippa filled in jerkily.

'What have you got against Andreo?'

'You're an Italian, aren't you?' Somewhat belatedly, Pippa connected his delicious growling accent to his likely nationality. Delicious? The dark timbre of his deep, low-pitched drawl was impossibly sexy. Thrown by the strange emergence of thoughts that seemed to have no direct input from her brain, she shifted off one foot onto the other. Without the smallest warning, she felt her nipples snap tight into stiff little buttons inside her bodice and her cheeks burned hot while she wondered what on earth was happening to her.

'I am.' Andreo continued to study her. No matter how hard or how long he studied her, her colouring was a source of continual fascination to him: that glowing cinnamon hair and those turquoise eyes enhanced by skin that had initially been pale as milk but that was now flaring a soft rose pink. It had been a long time since he had seen a woman blush and he was intrigued. 'You work for Venstar?'

Pippa nodded but she was extremely tense. 'You referred to Andreo D'Alessio as if you know him personally...'

He was Italian, Pippa was thinking in dismay. He had to work for D'Alessio and, if he was part of the initial wave of imported employees, he was unlikely to be a junior member of the team. Her tongue darted out in a nervous flicker over the soft underside of her lower lip.

Andreo found himself imagining that moist pink tip tracing an erotic path of exploration over his bared skin. The sudden throb of his aroused sex startled him for he was long past the teenage years when self-control in the radius of a beautiful woman had often been a challenge. 'Perhaps I'm just curious to know what you have against a man you've never met,' he breathed almost harshly.

Pippa tossed her head, cinnamon tresses spilling back against her slim white shoulders. Cautious as she was trying to be, it was already too late because the alcohol in her bloodstream was firing her every response with an unfamiliar aggression. 'How do you know I've never met him?'

Andreo elevated a fine black brow. 'You...*have*?'

'No, I haven't, but I don't need to meet him in the flesh to know that he's a sexist dinosaur, who discriminates against women to make himself feel more powerful!' Pippa slung bitterly.

CHAPTER TWO

DISCONCERTED, Andreo frowned down at the woman maligning his reputation as a fair employer. His ebony eyes glinted with golden highlights. He stifled an instinctive urge to slap her down so hard verbally that she would never again dare to make such an unjust charge against him. '*Dio mio*… That's a loaded accusation to make against a man whom you can know virtually nothing about.'

Pale as death and almost as taken aback as she could see he was by her angry outburst, Pippa dropped her head and muttered, 'Excuse me…'

As she began to move away Andreo swung round to effectively bar her passage. 'Don't rush away,' he urged.

What the heck had come over her? Pippa was asking herself in consternation. Only a mad woman would hurl an accusation like that about the boss at a work function! That wretched brandy had gone to her foolish head and loosened her tongue. Naturally she was bitter about the reasons why she had been passed over for promotion but, if she had no intention of making a formal complaint, she needed to keep her lips sealed for her own protection. 'Look, I—'

'You haven't even told me your name,' Andreo incised, noting the slight tremor of the pale slender hand she had braced against the wall.

After that crazy bout of outspokenness, only a suicidal idiot would gave a truthful response to a name, rank and number request that would identify her, Pippa conceded in dismay. Her head was beginning to pound in response to the increasing level of her stress. What was she to tell him? Pippa Plain? Pride brought up her head again as she remembered what her late mother had often called her. 'It's Philly…'

'Philly,' Andreo sounded out, rolling the syllables huskily together. 'I like it. Let me buy you a drink and convince you that Venstar's new owner walks on water even in his spare time—'

'Is he really that full of himself?' Pippa interrupted with aghast turquoise eyes.

'You have a problem with confident men?' In the act of frowning, Andreo again found himself questioning his own self-image.

'If by confident you mean arrogant, yes, I have a problem—'

'Andreo isn't arrogant. He is secure in himself and assertive,' Andreo pronounced with approval, ushering her in the direction of the quiet bar by dint of a light hand that only momentarily brushed her spine. 'But you must tell me why you referred to Andreo D'Alessio as sexist—'

Eager to avoid that controversial subject, Pippa murmured hurriedly, 'You haven't even told me your name yet…'

As if he already knew how much he off-balanced her, Andreo sent her a slanting grin.

Her heart hammered so hard and fast that she felt momentarily faint.

'It's Andreo, I'm afraid,' he supplied.

'Is that like…a common name in Italy?'

'Very much…every other guy is called Andreo,' Andreo groaned with silken mockery, surveying her from below the deceptively sleepy fringe of his black lashes, dark golden eyes vibrant with concealed amusement.

Pippa was fascinated, exhilarated and scared all at one and the same time. She had not even noticed him ordering a drink for her and when a waiter offered her a cocktail in a tall, thin glass she accepted it without comment and let the sparkling liquid moisten her throat.

'Are you married?' Pippa heard herself ask Andreo with all the effortless cool of a giant weight dropping from the sky. Having heard other women talk, she knew it was the one question that a sensible woman should always ask when she met a man for the first time.

He laughed out loud. 'You're so subtle...of course I'm not married. Tell me why you think Andreo D'Alessio is a dinosaur—'

'I don't want to talk about that.'

'I do.' Andreo stared down at her with the daunting force of will that came as naturally to his domineering nature as the need to breathe.

'I don't...' The tingle in the atmosphere gave Pippa a wicked thrill. She couldn't take her eyes off him and she felt as if she were locked into a live electric current.

Shimmering dark golden eyes rested on her. 'I'll get it out of you,' Andreo intoned with innate conviction in his own powers of persuasion. 'Do you always take shameless advantage of the fact that you're beautiful?'

Pippa spluttered on her drink and glanced up at him, riveted to the spot, her lovely eyes unguarded. 'Sorry...?'

He was chatting her up. She could hardly believe it. A guy who was a dead ringer for her ultimate fantasy male was flirting with her. And she didn't know how to handle it, had not a clue how to respond, so she smiled up at him, smiled and smiled and smiled, suddenly terrified that he might lose interest and walk away again. Wasn't it time she enjoyed what other women took for granted? Wasn't it time she took account of the reality that she was young and single? The admiration in his appreciative gaze was like a shot of adrenalin in her veins and balm to her wounded ego. Pippa Plain? *Who?*

That knowing feminine smile that appeared to suggest that she was aware of exactly the effect she was having on his libido tensed every muscle in Andreo's lean, powerful body. It had been a long time since sexual hunger had hit Andreo with that intensity and it had a mixed effect on him. Rigid with throbbing arousal, he wanted to behave like a caveman and thrust her back against the wall and crush those ripe coral lips under his again and again and again before he dragged her off somewhere much more private. But while his hot-blooded nature revelled in the rare heat of his desire for her, his intellect was in direct opposition. He liked to be in control, he *always* liked to be one hundred per cent in control.

'Santo Cielo,' he murmured thickly.

The ragged edge to his deep voice sent yet another responsive shiver travelling through Pippa. She meshed with scorching dark golden eyes and her mouth ran dry and her knees turned weak as water under her. For the first time in twenty three years she understood what it was like to be really wanted by a guy. And she didn't know *how* she understood, how she could possibly recognise the rough edge of desire stamping his lean, hard features and the passionate intensity of his stunning eyes. But although she had only just met him, she was attuned to his hunger with every humming fibre of her physical being. What she was feeling terrified her and excited her in equal parts.

'Let's get out of here...' Andreo breathed, deciding in

the space of a moment that he could plead a prior engagement to escape the party.

He extended a hand to her. She could not think straight but still she closed her fingers into his, unable to resist her own need to touch him. She quivered, tormented by the nagging ache she barely comprehended at the very heart of her body, and stared down at their linked hands while she strove to get a grip on herself again.

'This is crazy,' she mumbled shakily.

Andreo's mobile phone sounded up the tune his fourteen-year-old kid brother had fed into it to announce that he and *only* he was calling. Anybody else calling at that instant would have been ignored but Andreo was always ruefully aware that in the eyes of Marco, who was less than half his own age, he had more the standing of a father than a brother.

Even white teeth gritting, Andreo released Pippa's hand with an apology for the interruption and dug out his phone to answer it. His sibling plunged straight into outlining the mathematics question he was struggling to answer. Suppressing a groan of disbelief, Andreo flipped over a flyer lying on the bar counter and jotted down the problem on the blank side of the sheet.

'My little brother…he's in boarding school and sometimes he needs a hand with his work,' he explained tautmouthed to Pippa.

Blinking, only slowly emerging from the daze induced by her own screaming hormones and her wild response to Andreo, Pippa hovered by his side. She was shattered by the acknowledgement that she had been on the very brink of going off with Andreo. A guy she had only just met, a guy she knew nothing about! She was incredulous at her own reckless behaviour and appalled. Anyone might have been forgiven for thinking that she had lost her wits the same moment she'd first laid eyes on Andreo!

'Marco…' Andreo could feel Pippa's sudden withdrawal as much as if she had slammed a door shut in his face. He had to fight to keep the exasperated edge from his intonation as his impatient little brother asked him how long it would take for him to solve the problem for him.

In the act of emerging from shock to plunge into embarrassment instead as she wondered how the heck she was to retain Andreo's interest while also telling him that she had changed her mind about going any place with him, Pippa noticed that Andreo was in the act of striving to differentiate trigonometric functions on the flyer.

'That line's in error,' she muttered with a slight frown as she drew closer to him.

Andreo froze in astonishment. 'Is that a fact?' he challenged.

Pippa filched the pen from between his fingers and at lightning speed ran through the question to emerge with the answer while at the same time succinctly explaining where he had gone wrong in his calculations.

Andreo breathed in very deep and slow. He was better than ninety-nine out of a hundred people at maths and he had just met the hundredth in the unexpected guise of a very lovely and tactless redhead. Was he a chauvinist bastard?

'Andreo…' Marco breathed in wonderment, having overheard the entire dialogue and haltered by no such reservations. 'Whoever she is she's a real whiz at this stuff. Not one of your usual airheads, is she? Make sure you get her phone number for me!'

As Andreo finished the call it occurred to Pippa that she had not been very diplomatic. Tabby, who seemed to have been born knowing how the male mind worked, had once told her that men had very tender egos and that, if you really, really liked a guy, you should always leave him space to save face. Aware that she had steamrollered over him, she almost winced.

Over the top of her head, Andreo saw two members of his personal staff lurking by the door of the conference hall, visibly anxious to rope him back into the festivities but understandably reluctant to interrupt him and his companion. He pressed her round the corner of the bar where they were no longer within view.

'We should separate and return to the hall for ten or fifteen minutes…practise discretion,' Andreo ground out half under his breath, while gazing stormily down into her beautiful face, his reluctance to part from her palpable, 'but I don't want to let you out of my sight for a second in case I lose you, *cara*.'

Unaccustomed to being treated like a *femme fatale* whom no mere male could resist, Pippa just giggled, convinced that he was teasing her. Hands snapping to her elbows, Andreo backed her into the phone cubicle behind her and hauled her close.

'What are you doing?' she gasped in stark disconcertion.

'What do you want me to do?' Andreo enquired in a husky, ragged undertone, languorous golden eyes hot with invitation on hers.

Held in intimate contact with every lean, hard angle of his big, powerful frame, Pippa discovered in shock that she just wanted to be even closer to him, indeed so close that she might qualify as an extra layer of his skin. This time around she understood why her breasts felt heavy and almost swollen. She recognised her own desire for him and her face burned with mortification but nothing could kill the raw, wicked longing quivering through her in a thousand tiny stinging needles as her body came alive in ways entirely new to her.

'Philly…?'

Tempted beyond all bearing by promptings that she had never been forced to deal with before, Pippa let her arms slide up to link round his strong brown neck and eased closer into the hard, unyielding strength of him. With a stifled Italian curse, Andreo succumbed to that frank invitation with all the volatile passion that lay at the heart of his nature.

Pippa might have been new to passion but no victim could have been more eager to seek her fate. He took her softly parted lips under his and thrust them apart with the forceful onslaught of his. The sweet, unbearably rousing invasion of his tongue into the moist interior of her mouth made her heart give a heavy thud and tightened her every muscle. All of a sudden her entire body was alive and throbbing with near-painful excitement and greedy for more of what she had never had.

With a reflexive shudder at the amount of strength it demanded from him and rigid with fierce desire, Andreo yanked himself back from her. Heavily lidded golden eyes swept her bemused face and lingered on the soft, swollen red of her ripe mouth. 'Ten minutes…and you stay within view the whole time,' he warned thickly. 'Then we leave together.'

Blinking like a woman emerging from a dark spell of enchantment, Pippa let herself be walked back across the foyer and finally into the busy hall. The clumps of chattering people seemed to evaporate from their path at magical speed and Andreo only came to a halt when they reached a vacant corner table. There he snapped his fingers to hail a passing waiter and order her a drink.

Momentarily, his imperious show of command took her aback.

'Now don't move from here until I come back, *cara mia*,' Andreo instructed in a low-pitched drawl. 'It would be so easy for us to lose each other in this crush.'

'Are you worth waiting for?' Pippa heard herself enquire in a teasing undertone for she could only be amused at being spoken to as though she were a feckless child likely to wander off and get lost without his guidance.

'Don't laugh. This is not funny.' Andreo was angry that she could seem unconcerned at the same risk and equally infuriated by his own lack of cool. He wanted her. But the level of that wanting was already more than he felt comfortable with. As his mobile phone broke into Marco's colourful signature tune again, he worked out how best to pin her down in the short term.

'Do you think you could help my little brother with his homework again?' he asked. 'He speaks excellent English.'

Touched by that request, Pippa grinned and extended her hand for his phone. Sipping at her drink, she talked Marco through what remained of his assignment while she watched Andreo on the other side of the room watch her in turn. Every time she saw that proud dark head angle in her direction, scorching dark golden eyes burning up the distance between them, her mouth ran dry and her heart raced. Venstar bigwigs surrounded him and the portly little man she had earlier identified as D'Alessio, but in that almost anonymous sea of people she was conscious of only one very individual male: Andreo.

Everything she was feeling was so outrageously new to her. Nothing had ever seemed so wonderful and miraculous as the simple fact that Andreo appeared to be as impressed by her as she was by him. No matter how hard she tried to reclaim her usual sterling common sense, it was overwhelmed by the outrageously girlish giddy excitement leaping and dancing through her bloodstream.

She had not known a guy *could* kiss like that. She had not known that a guy could actually make her feel like that. Oh, yes, she had heard women describe certain men as irresistible, but she had scorned the belief that any male could have such an extreme effect on her. But even while she had disbelieved those claims, she had always secretly longed to be proven wrong, she acknowledged dizzily. And when Andreo had kissed her every skin cell in her body had responded with breathtaking enthusiasm. All that had kept her upright was the reality that she had had her arms wrapped round him and he was strong enough to bear her weight.

While she studied Andreo from afar her blue eyes sparkled with wondering satisfaction when he immediately directed his gaze to her as though some sixth sense had warned him of her appraisal. His charismatic smile set fireworks off inside her tummy and made her heart thump as frantically fast as though she had run a marathon.

'Will you give me your phone number?' Marco prompted in a wheedling tone. 'You're much better at explaining this stuff than Andreo is.'

Lounging back against the edge of the table, her burnished fall of hair fiery as flames against her fair, delicate skin, the vibrant blue dress a simple understated frame for her superb long-legged figure, Pippa was attracting a great deal of both male and female attention. But not one of the star-struck men admiring her would have dared to approach her while Andreo D'Alessio watched her with such blatant possessiveness in his arrogant gaze and a flashing intimate smile on his firm, hard mouth.

Pippa had just finished talking to Marco when Andreo rejoined her. Drawing level with her, he barely broke his stride as he closed a lean brown hand over hers to urge her towards the exit. She heard the buzz of speculative voices break out as they passed by together. But then he was incredibly handsome and, as nobody had approached her while she'd been alone at the table, it seemed fair to assume that none of her colleagues had recognised her without her curls, her spectacles and her serviceable suits.

When the lift doors closed on them, she leant back against the cool metal wall because the fresh air-conditioned atmosphere was making her head swim to a dismaying degree.

'You still haven't told me why you suspect Andreo D'Alessio of being prejudiced against women in the workplace…'

In disconcertion, Pippa blinked. 'I thought you'd have forgotten about that by now—'

'I never forget anything,' Andreo confided.

'Well, do your best to forget that,' Pippa mumbled ruefully. 'I was indiscreet—'

'You can trust me,' Andreo purred.

'A little bird told me your namesake—'

'My namesake? The little guy who reminded you of a leprechaun?'

Reassured by that light-hearted sally, Pippa nodded and tried with some difficulty to concentrate. 'The word is that the big boss only likes pretty women to make it up the promotion ladder—'

'That's a four-letter word, *cara*!' Andreo incised in bold disagreement.

When it came to their mutual employer, he was evidently very strong on the loyalty front. As that was an old-fashioned quality that she admired, she could not

think less of him for it. Lashes carefully lowered, for she
wanted the topic closed, she murmured soothingly, 'I'm
sure you're right.'

'I know I'm right.' Andreo continued with conviction.
Pippa almost smiled at his absolute certainty.

Andreo reached out and used her own hands to draw
her close to him again. 'I like the way you feel against
me, *carissima*...'

Powerfully aware of his abrasive masculinity and the
hard muscular strength of him, she rested against him,
suddenly weak with wanting. 'Me too...I mean, I like
being close to you too.'

He laughed with husky appreciation, slid long fingers
into the thick fall of her hair to tug her head back and
look at her again. Beneath the harsh lights in the lift, the
clarity of her blue eyes mesmerised him for he could read
every passing thought: the shy uncertainty laced with the
stubborn bravado of her pride and deeper still...the feverish hunger for him that she could not hide.

He devoured her mouth with an urgency that left her
reeling. She could not spare the time or the energy to
breathe and she lost herself in the earthy taste of him,
revelling in the eagerness of her own desire. When he
straightened to walk her out of the lift again, she let her
head rest against his broad shoulder while she drank in
air to aid her starved lungs.

Her mind was in turmoil. She could barely believe that
what she was feeling was real but was at the same time
impossibly greedy - for that no-longer-connected-to-
planet-earth sensation to continue. He employed a card
to open a door that led into a very luxurious suite.

Not having until that moment taken the time to consider *where* he was taking her, Pippa was aghast to appreciate that he had accommodation in the hotel itself and

that she had unthinkingly allowed him to bring her back up there with him.

'Are you expecting me to stay the night with you?' Pippa demanded in dismay.

CHAPTER THREE

ANDREO dealt Pippa a level challenging appraisal. 'That's entirely your decision.'

Colour swept Pippa's face and she could have bitten her tongue out in embarrassment. Of course that was *her* decision! It was a good half-century since women had been raised to think that what a man expected a woman should invariably try to deliver. She walked over to the tall windows that overlooked the spectacular city skyline but she could only think of how foolish she must have sounded to him. Like a nervous virgin who had never been alone with a man in a hotel suite before? All the heat drained from below her fair skin to leave her pale.

Unfortunately, Hilary had only managed to make her over on the outside with a smooth sophisticated façade and inside she was still the same old Pippa Stevenson, she acknowledged. Pippa, who had attended an all girls' school and whose evenings and weekends had been filled with extra classes and academic study, rather than social events and flirting. Boys had always seemed as remote and strange to her as alien entities and she had never learned what to say or how to behave around them. At the age of seventeen she had been humiliated by the young man she'd been infatuated with and, from that day on, hurt pride had become her strongest source of protection.

Time might have moved on but once bitten twice shy had proved to be her motto. Since then she might as well have been living on a single sex planet, she conceded ruefully, for she had never again risked pain or rejection. For almost six years she had been her father's carer and while it was true that the older man had demanded that she devote all her free time to his needs and his interests, it was equally true that she had not offered much of a protest. It had been easier to be a dutiful daughter and accept without question that she was the 'big strapping lass' her parent had often called her and highly unlikely to appeal to any man. From the age of twelve, when she had first shot up in height to tower over all her classmates like a lanky beanpole, Pippa had loathed her extra inches and had pointlessly longed to be small and dainty like her pretty mother.

But now, for the first time, she shook free of that memory without regret and reminded herself that Andreo appeared to admire her just as she was. She stole a covert glance at him and collided with smouldering dark golden eyes and her mouth ran dry. He was breathtakingly handsome.

Andreo watched her, for she was so still that she might have been a living breathing statue. Her feathery lashes lowered above the pale perfect line of her cheekbones and she looked incredibly vulnerable. It was obvious that she was having second thoughts. Was there another guy in her life? Someone to whom she felt she owed loyalty? Whatever, he chose patience over the risk of losing her altogether. 'Perhaps I should just take you home,' he murmured evenly.

Pippa went rigid, for that unexpected offer only heightened her tension. Go home? It would be the sensible thing to do. Yet her whole being rebelled against the concept. *Sensible* Pippa. When had she ever been anything else? And where had it got her? She had become a workaholic with no social life and no man had looked twice at her either. When had she ever felt for any male what she was feeling now?

'Is there anyone else?' Andreo breathed, his tension palpable.

'No...' She drew in a slow steadying breath. 'You?'

'No.' The blonde who had last shared Andreo's bed was modelling in Mexico and he saw no reason to confess that the lady had become yesterday's news at the exact same instant that he'd seen her successor before him.

The atmosphere buzzed.

'I don't believe that I've ever wanted any woman as much as I want you, *bella mia*,' Andreo confided with raw honesty.

'I want to stay...' Pippa whispered in a rush and, shaken though she was by the force of her own craving for him, she was equally entrapped by the simple acknowledgement that she still had a whole new dimension of life to explore. Her body seemed to be developing responses all of its own. The fabric of her dress felt abrasive against the taut peaks of her breasts and there was a swollen heaviness low in her pelvis that made it a challenge for her to remain still.

'You won't regret it.' His slashing smile of satisfaction was sufficient reward for her agreement. Her heart hammered so hard inside her ribcage that she felt dizzy. He was so beautiful and when he looked at her she felt beautiful too. She crossed the room on lower limbs that felt as unreliable in the support stakes as bendy twigs. She was trembling but she reached for his silk tie like a woman who meant business, a woman who knew exactly what she was doing.

Averse to her clumsy approach, his wretched tie refused to cooperate and went into a tight, immoveable knot. Just when she was on the brink of screaming for a pair of scissors, lean brown fingers intervened and jerked loose the knot with apparent ease. He cast the tie aside and drew her raised hands into his own to fold her back into his arms. She was as boneless as a rag doll until he crushed her into the hard, muscular wall of his chest, one masculine hand knotting into her bright hair to angle her head back. Then she shivered, stretched up to him, helpless in the thrall of her own wild anticipation.

His expert mouth swooped down to taste hers again and a soft moan of encouragement broke low in her throat. He traced her lips, penetrated them and a series of little gasps were torn from her as she clung to him to stay upright. He bent down and swept her up into his arms.

'Aren't I too heavy?' she mumbled through swollen, stinging lips and a sense of wonderment as dangerous as a hypnotic spell. He was, she was convinced, 'the one', the one special guy who she had always hoped and prayed might be waiting out there for her. The guy she was going to fall madly in love with. The guy who was hopefully going to fall madly in love with her. Well, maybe not madly, she adjusted hurriedly, fearful of hoping for too much and ending up with precisely nothing as a punishment for daring to be so ambitious. Even if he fell just a little bit in love with her, she would be content, she swore to herself.

'Light as a doll, *cara mia*…I'm just an unrepentant show-off,' Andreo teased as he strode into the elegant contemporary bedroom next door and set her down again onto her own feet.

One of her shoes had fallen off and she kicked off the other, but he had already stepped back from her to unbutton his shirt. Eyes wide, she became his audience. Her toes curled in the luxury carpet while she watched as the shirt fell open to display a sleek bronze wedge of masculine torso, his powerful pectoral muscles delineated by a triangle of rough dark curls. Her tummy flipped and she felt alarmingly short of breath and very hot. Knees wobbling, she backed up until her legs hit the edge of the bed and she sank down on the luxurious mattress.

'What…?' A wicked smile slanted over his wide, sensual mouth and golden eyes gleamed from below dense black lashes. 'Did you want to take off the shirt for me?'

'No…er…I'm not into shirts,' Pippa framed, dry-mouthed and serious, for she had decided there was nothing less cool than struggling with male apparel.

'You can always practise on my tie, *cara*,' Andreo teased with intense amusement for he had found her lack of dexterity and the inexperience implied by that trait endearing.

'Is that a fact?' Pippa strove to match his mood with a quip while acknowledging that his sheer masculine presence both thrilled and intimidated her.

'Any time…' Andreo husked, strolling forward with all the formidable and yet daunting grace of a prowling tiger to lean down and close his large hands over her smaller ones and raise her upright.

That close to him her nostrils flared on the clean, husky male scent of his lithe, lean physique. She quivered, a curl of heat igniting low in her stomach. Shorn of her shoes as she now was, he struck her as awesomely tall and broad.

'*Santo Cielo*…you've shrunk a little,' Andreo mocked. 'But promise me that you will always wear those heels around me. Seeing you top all the guys around me gives me a high—'

'It…*does?*'

'*Sì*. You looked as disdainful as a queen too.' He shed his shirt and reached behind her with complete calm to unzip her dress for her.

'Couldn't we put the lights out?' Pippa mumbled in as humorous a tone as she could manage, the cooler air brushing her spine merely reminding her that when the dress went she had only one more layer left to hide behind.

Andreo actually laughed out loud. 'You've got to be kidding, *bella mia*!'

Perspiration beaded her short upper lip. 'I guess I was…'

He skimmed the straps down from her taut shoulders and let her slinky little blue dress fall to the carpet. He spread long fingers to frame her cheekbones. 'You are stunning…'

But Pippa had already closed her eyes sooner than risk seeing his disappointment when he saw how thin and flat-chested she was when stripped back to her bra and briefs. Nerves strung high, she shivered and he gathered her up into his arms and came down onto the bed with her cradled across his hard thighs. He tasted her mouth long and slow and the forbidden heat in her tummy flickered up again in spite of her tension.

'Sexy…' Andreo growled, appreciating the satin-smooth softness of her delicate white skin.

Nobody had ever called her that before and the temptation was too great: her lashes lifted on bemused eyes as blue as sapphires. 'Sexy?'

'Very…' He found everything about her sexy: her hair, her eyes, her height, her incandescent smile, the air of fragility that she exuded that gave him a curious urge to open doors for her, the sort of courteous but unfashionable stuff he normally only did in the radius of his female relatives.

Mesmerised by the intensity of his dark golden appraisal, she missed out on the deft movement with which he unclipped her bra. 'Honestly…?'

As her firm little breasts were bared his breathing fractured. Air chilled the tightly beaded tips and she looked down at her own bare flesh in dismay before bringing her hands up to cover herself from his intent appraisal. 'Lights…' she said in a wobbly voice.

'I love your body…' Andreo told her.

Feverish colour flooded her cheeks as she scrambled off him and dived with more haste than elegance below the fancy quilted spread and tugged it back up to her chin.

Andreo elevated a level dark brow and surveyed her with a frown. Her cinnamon hair was fanned out like polished silk round her face, which was hot pink to her hairline. Her eyes were evasive.

'I think I need a drink,' she gasped, amazed that after all the alcohol she had imbibed she still felt almost as sober as the proverbial judge.

Andreo sprang upright and strolled over to the mini bar to withdraw a chilled mineral water. Opening it, he emptied it into a crystal tumbler and wandered back to extend it to her.

Clutching the spread to her, Pippa accepted the glass. She did not have the nerve to tell him that she had expected to receive an alcoholic beverage. 'You must be thinking I'm a little strange,' she muttered in a rush.

'Why would I think that?' Drinking water from the bottle he had helped himself to, Andreo rested his lean hips on the edge of the cabinet opposite while he contemplated her tense and embarrassed face.

No way was she having another intoxicating drink. He liked his partners to know what day it was. But there was another guy in her life, he was sure of it. That was why she was so jumpy. His competitive spirit soared into the ascendant. He would talk his way into that bed with her tonight. He might only get this one chance to pull her and once the deed was done, it would squash the competition. And if she didn't squash the competition after the event, he most assuredly would take care of that necessity for her. He didn't share and she was his. *Dio mio*, never before had he kissed a woman in a public bar or been so challenged to restrain his overwhelming hunger to possess her. Together they were hotter than a volcano and if she didn't yet appreciate that fact, he would soon teach her to do so.

The silence stretched and with the galling cool of an expert interrogator he made no attempt to break it.

Pippa sat up in a driven motion and hugged the spread beneath her arms. 'There's something I ought to mention…'

Andreo tensed. He really did not want to hear about the other man. Everything she told him would linger in his memory and annoy him. He didn't know how he knew that. He didn't even know why he was thinking that, for he had never been one of those weird possessive types. But he did know that he did not want to hear the low-down on her soon-to-be-ex-boyfriend. 'I don't believe in exchanging stories about other lovers.'

'Neither do I…and I'm not even sure I should make such an issue of this…but—' Pippa sucked in a jerky breath and shot him an anxious glance '—it seems only fair to warn you that I haven't done this much.'

Andreo was touched. He didn't want to hurt her pride so there was no easy way of telling her that she had made her relative lack of experience pretty obvious. He was fine with that. But then he was a very open-minded guy, he reflected.

'In fact...' Pippa hesitated, worrying at her full lower lip with her teeth, her quiet voice dropping lower and lower in level until he was leaning forward without realising it to catch her words. '...to be really, *really* frank, I haven't done this at all...'

His winged black brows pleated. 'Say that again...'

'Ever,' Pippa concluded.

'You're telling me that you've never spent the night with a guy you've just met before?'

'Yes, but not just that,' Pippa interposed a shade irritably for he was being exceedingly slow on the uptake when she wanted him to get the message faster than the speed of light. 'Apart from the fact that I'm not promiscuous—'

'Hey...hold it there, I was not making a judgement,' Andreo slotted in, lying in his teeth for he never, ever got involved with women who slept around.

'But that...well, that I've never slept with a guy before...I'm, er, you know...' Pippa shot an almost pleading glance at Andreo but, while showing every sign of granting her one hundred per cent of his attention, he did not seem about to help her out '...a virgin...'

'A...a what?' Andreo frowned in evident bewilderment. 'Did you just say what I thought you said?'

Bearing a close resemblance to a stone image at that point, Pippa nodded, twin high spots of self-conscious colour blooming over her cheekbones. He looked really shocked and she had not been prepared for that reaction.

'But you're not a teenager.' Andreo seemed to be sinking into deeper shock with every second that passed.

'So?'

A virgin. She was a virgin. He was blowing it. He ought to be taking this confession in his stride, not staring at her as if she had just leapt fully formed out of a medieval painting. She looked so anxious and she was blushing like mad and something inside him just twisted. In one bold movement, he rose upright and moved forward to come down on the bed beside her.

'It's not a problem,' Andreo asserted, fishing below the spread to gather her back into his arms but with rather more circumspection that he had utilised moments earlier.

It was not a problem, he told himself. Why should it be a problem?

'Honestly?' she pressed unevenly.

Lust fought with innate decency inside Andreo and the guy he liked to think he was surfaced for the first time in longer than he cared to recall. 'You need to think about this—'

'No, I don't.' Pippa closed her arms tightly round him and resisted the urge to scream that she had spent all her adult years thinking and thinking and thinking and hardly ever just *doing*. The very feel of his long, lean body next to hers made her heart speed up. She gazed into dark golden eyes enhanced by spiky black lashes and breathing normally became a distinct challenge. In fact just looking at him unleashed a flock of butterflies in her tummy and that was followed up by a wanton, warm, melting sensation that pierced deep enough to make her blush and squirm.

'Why me?' Andreo framed, inching down the spread while he kept her preoccupied and burying his hungry mouth against the delicate ridge of her collar-bone where a tiny pulse was flickering like crazy. The very scent of her soft skin enthralled him.

Jerking, she gasped in oxygen like a drowning swimmer and then buried her face in the cropped luxuriance of his black hair. Her entire body was humming like a race car engine revving up and she couldn't concentrate. 'I don't know…'

'Yes, you do…' Andreo countered.

And he was right, she registered in dim surprise. She wanted him more than she had ever wanted anything or anybody: it *was* that basic.

Andreo thrust the spread from his path and paused to admire the succulent pink nipples he had uncovered. 'You're exquisite…' And he rubbed those stiff, swollen buds with knowing fingers before lowering his dark head to lave them with his tongue.

Her spine arched up to him and she cried out in sensual shock at the sheer intensity of sensation. Her fingers dug into his hair and she flung her head back. He toyed with the tender tips while he kissed her again with erotic thoroughness, very much a male staking a claim and taking his time. She wrapped her arms tight round him, crushing her sensitised, tingling breasts into the hard, abrasive wall of his chest and letting her hands trace the breadth of his muscular shoulders and the long, silky smooth line of his strong back.

'I promise I'll make it good, *cara,*' Andreo swore, pulling back from her and springing upright to shed his well cut trousers.

Soft mouth voluptuous and red from the hungry urgency of his, she stared at him. From his superb torso to his taut, flat stomach, lean hips and powerful thighs, he was all hard muscle and sleek bronzed skin: magnificently male. His boxer shorts could not conceal the virile evidence of his male arousal. Untouched by an atom of her self-conscious shyness, he skimmed off that final garment and all the curiosity she had never owned up to possessing was fully met. Eyes wide, face burning, she dropped her head again. For goodness' sake, how on earth…?

He tossed back the spread beneath which she had again taken refuge. She connected with smouldering dark golden eyes and suddenly she was stretching up to welcome him back to her, her body tight and hot and restive in ways she did not even understand.

'How virginal is virginal?' Andreo husked.

'On a scale of one to ten…ten being the ultimate…probably almost ten,' she said breathlessly.

'Your skin is as translucent as porcelain.' Andreo explored the pert mounds of her small breasts, lingered to tease her distended pink nipples with his expert mouth. 'You're so delicate, so sensitive there. I love that.'

She couldn't lie still beneath his ministrations. Heart thundering, she arched into his caresses, eager for more, shameless in pursuit of that ever more seductive pleasure that built and built to a level that was almost a torment. 'Kiss me…'

He savoured her lips, let his tongue tangle with hers, laughed with earthy appreciation as she dragged him down to her with impatient hands, hungry for the weight of him over her, the firm, hard pressure of his mouth, and denied it.

'You said you'd never wanted anyone as much as me…' she reminded him shakily. 'Was that a lie?'

'I want you to feel the same passion but you're too impatient,' Andreo growled, sliding a hand beneath her restive legs to tug up her knees and remove her briefs. 'We have all night, *bella mia*.'

Her hips shifted against the sheet as she sought helplessly to quell the ache at the very centre of her. She was insanely aware of every sensitised inch of her throbbing body: the straining buds of her breasts still wet from his attentions, the swollen dampness between her thighs. She pushed up against his big, powerful frame, adoring the unyielding contours of bone and rippling muscle below his bronzed skin, wildly conscious of the rock-hard rigidity of his bold erection.

Golden eyes glittering, Andreo lifted away from her as though she had burned him, aggressive jaw-line set at an angle. 'I intend this to be special.'

It was as if a fever had hold of her and her temperature were out of control. She wanted so desperately to touch him and all that had been holding her back was fear of doing something wrong. She headed back into the heat and strength of him and let her mouth trail from a muscular shoulder down over his hair-roughened chest. There she paused to snatch in an erratic breath and lick and kiss her path across his taut ribcage where…he closed his hand into her hair and dragged her back up to him before she could really start experimenting.

'Independent woman,' he whispered in a tone of raw discovery.

He was a control freak but he was gorgeous, she thought dizzily. She studied the black hair she had disarranged, the riveting eyes, high, proud cheekbones, arrogant nose and classic and willful masculine mouth and inside she turned boneless. 'So I'll lie back and think of…?'

'Me…you think about *me*,' Andreo instructed with complete seriousness and he kissed her and refused to consider why he had said something so naff.

He reacquainted himself with her slender, seductive curves. In the process, she gasped air in shallow bursts and he forced her to stop thinking and just feel and what she felt was extraordinary in its very intensity. His fingers flirted with the damp curls at the junction of her slim, restive thighs and she moaned out loud, her hips rising off the mattress in a yearning movement as old as time.

'Oh, please…!' she gasped.

At last, he touched her where she most needed to be touched, exploring the moist, silken heat at the heart of her where the ache was a torment. Heat and wanton pleasure engulfed her as he utilised a lean finger to probe her tight depths, opening her for his skilled caresses until she felt like honey heated to boiling point and on the brink of spontaneous combustion. It was the sweetest torture she had ever withstood because just when she believed the heights of pleasure could not climb any higher, he would prove her wrong.

'I'm mad for you,' Andreo groaned, rising over her and tipping her back from him in one smooth motion.

She felt him, hard and smooth and demanding, enter her. The sharp, rending pain took her aback and her blue eyes flew wide in dismay.

Andreo stilled as a whimper of protest was dredged from her. 'Shall I stop?'

'No…' There was too much of him and she had known that and she shut her eyes tight, waiting until the pain of his intrusion had lessened yet savouring the wonderfully erotic feel of him inside her.

'I don't think I'm supposed to be enjoying myself this much when you're not,' he muttered in ragged masculine apology.

And she almost laughed and knew beyond a shadow of a doubt that she was going to fall in love with him if she hadn't already. 'It's OK…' she whispered shakily.

'*Amore*…' Andreo pressed his lips to her damp brow. 'You're very brave—'

'Greedy for you,' she confided guiltily, rising up to

him to invite a deeper invasion, controlled by her own desperate need for fulfillment.

He surged into her again and she arched and gasped in shock at the rich, sensual tide of sensation. He prolonged her pleasure with every art he had ever learned. Hot and hungry for him, she succumbed to his pagan rhythm with helpless abandon. The burn low in her pelvis had become a tight knot of delirious excitement, dragging her higher and higher until her heart was thundering in her ears. She hit a pinnacle and drowning pleasure rocked her with wave after wave of ecstasy. As he drove himself into a shuddering release, she held him tight, dazed and oddly proud and incredibly happy. She had had a wonderful time trashing her sensible former self and she had not a single regret.

She dozed off to sleep without realising it. Sliding back into bed, Andreo shook her awake again. 'It's only midnight,' he told her in teasing reproof. 'How can you be so tired this early?'

Snuggling back into him, Pippa went pink and avoided his too-shrewd gaze. She knew that it had to be the amount of alcohol she had consumed that was making her brain feel as if it were filled with cotton wool and her eyelids behave as though they had lead weights attached to them. 'Sorry…'

Andreo arranged her back against the pillow and smoothed her tumbled hair back from her brows. 'What we just shared was fantastic for me but I have a confession to make…'

Her lashes swept up on his serious expression and her heart sank. 'You're married?'

'Dio mio…'

His angry look of reproof soothed her fears so she

moved to what was the next-worst scenario in her mind. 'Cheating on your girlfriend?'

'I don't cheat,' Andreo declared loftily, choosing to overlook the reality that a purist might deem him still, in the strictest sense, involved with Lili because he flatly refused to dump anyone by phone.

'Then what…?'

He grimaced. 'The condom broke. Too much enthusiasm on my part…I very much doubt that there will be any repercussions but I thought I ought to warn you.'

Pippa lay very still. 'The…er…*broke*?'

Andreo employed several rather more apt and descriptive expressions that made her face heat with embarrassment.

'I have a clean bill of health. No need to worry about that angle. I've always taken precautions,' he continued levelly. 'But obviously there is a risk that I could have made you pregnant.'

The very sound of that unexpected word, 'pregnant', shook Pippa rigid. An embarrassed little laugh escaped her because she could not begin to imagine so far-reaching a consequence as a little baby resulting from a defective condom. 'I'm sure I'll be fine…it's not that easy to get pregnant. There's two women in my section attending an infertility clinic,' she extended in a rush of abstracted confidence. 'It seems that these days quite a few women have problems conceiving.'

When Pippa had laughed, Andreo's blue-shadowed aggressive jaw-line had clenched. 'The women who marry into my family don't have problems of that nature.'

Pippa pushed her face into a bare brown muscular shoulder to hide her helpless grin. So, he was the contemporary equivalent of a caveman, who confused fertility with virility, was he? That was so sweet. She had to resist an inexplicable urge to hug him tight. 'Are you fond of children?' she asked, her amusement suffering a sudden check.

'I'm one of five…what do you think?'

He was ducking the issue but, just as her amusement had vanished, she had no desire to probe more deeply. She had only been ten years old when she had decided that she wouldn't ever want to have children. In her teen years, she had been quite open about the fact but had too often found herself under attack and forced to defend what were essentially private views on the subject. He might well feel as she did, mightn't he? Perhaps he had had a miserable childhood as well and, like her, shrank from the risk of inflicting similar suffering on a child of his own…

Andreo attempted to read her tranquil expression for he had discovered that for the first time in his life he was extraordinarily impatient to hear a woman's opinion on a topic he usually avoided like the plague. He almost groaned out loud when he registered that it was the tranquillity of sleep that had reclaimed her. He recalled her patience with his decidedly irritating little brother and he found himself smiling. He was willing to bet that she was crazy about kids.

Furthermore, why had he been worrying when she was patently unconcerned by that unfortunate glitch with the condom? What did she know that he didn't? Most probably, he decided, she was too shy to tell him that at the current stage of her cycle there was precious little chance of conception having taken place.

Pippa wakened to the sound of her mobile buzzing only inches away from her head.

While acknowledging that she had a headache and felt

as though she had engaged in some very over-active sport, she fumbled for the phone and half sat up to answer it. 'Hmm?'

'Did you sleep well, *bella mia*?' an awesomely familiar masculine drawl enquired in a tone as smooth as black velvet.

At the same time, Pippa struggled to adjust to the additional revelation that she was stark naked and lying in a bed in an only vaguely familiar hotel room. 'S-sorry?' she stammered.

'I ordered breakfast for you,' Andreo continued with quiet assurance. 'It should be waiting for you next door about now.'

Dazed blue eyes now huge and appalled, Pippa stared down at the phone in her hand and blinked rapidly. 'I thought maybe…er…maybe I dreamt you up,' she confided unsteadily.

'Your dreams are that exciting?' Andreo teased in an intimate undertone, flagrantly ignoring signals from his personal staff that his presence was awaited in the boardroom.

'For goodness' sake…what time is it?' Pippa exclaimed.

'Half-past nine, sleepyhead…but don't worry, I'm happy to give you the day off.' A reflective smile on his wide, sensual mouth, Andreo was picturing her as he had seen her before he'd left his suite. All tousled and flushed and beautiful even while still asleep. She had been exhausted, he recalled. She should spend the day in bed recouping her energies.

'Half-past *nine*? A day off…are you kidding?' Pippa framed in a rather high-pitched response.

'We're dining out tonight and I want you to be rested,'

Andreo countered with all the masterful cool of a male who felt it was his business to ensure her well-being.

Had she signed over her soul to him as well as her body the night before? She flinched in shame and growing shock. 'Andreo…I appreciate that you have to be senior to me at Venstar but I don't take days off just because I'm tired—'

'But you will today, *cara*,' Andreo intoned, waving away the executives hovering in the doorway with a censorious frown as he concentrated on his call.

'Why?' she whispered shakily.

'Why?' Andreo queried in frank astonishment for, in his own opinion, he had only made a tiny request. 'If for no other reason then to please me, of course!'

Since when had pleasing a guy been one of her priorities? Since you fell for tall, dark and domineering, who wasn't a dream last night!

'Look, it's not convenient for me to chat right now. But I have a surprise to share with you tonight over dinner. I think it'll make you smile. Leave me your address so that I know where to pick you up,' he instructed before he concluded the call.

Oh, boy, was he in for a surprise! No way was she taking a day off the same day that Cheryl assumed management of the finance section. Shaking her buzzing head, Pippa set her phone down and then as swiftly snatched it up again. As it was already after nine, she needed to call work and make her excuses before saying when she *would* be in. Calculating how long it was likely to take her to travel home and get changed before trailing all the way back across the city to begin work at around lunchtime if she was lucky, Pippa winced and abandoned that idea. Almost throwing herself out of bed, she raced about picking up her clothing and hurtled into the bathroom. It would be faster and simpler if she simply *bought* a new outfit to wear!

Into the shower she went, determined to think of nothing but her goal of getting into work as fast as possible, but her self-discipline crumpled while she washed. Every movement reminded her of the intimate ache at the heart of her body from Andreo's passionate possession. She was torn between mortification and a guilty sensation of happiness that seemed wholly inappropriate in the circumstances. Alcohol had banished her caution and her inhibitions and she had gone to bed with a male she had only just met. His interest had turned her head and she was shocked at the speed and ease with which her pride and moral principles had fallen in the face of temptation. Hadn't she behaved like a tramp?

But she discovered that she could not be that hard on herself. Not every romance was strictly conventional, she told herself urgently. Andreo seemed as wildly attracted to her as she was to him and he had called her first thing and he wanted to take her out to dinner that very evening. Reaching for the towel as she left the shower, she saw her reflection in the mirror and wrinkled her nose at the dizzy grin on her own face. All right, so he was gorgeous, she bargained with herself, but wasn't that all the more reason to make an effort to keep her foolish feet on the ground?

Fully dressed and having paused only to print her address on the writing pad by the bed, she entered the elegant reception room next door and came to a startled halt. An exquisite arrangement of roses adorned with an envelope carrying the name 'Philly' met her attention first. Even as she breathed in the glorious scent of the wonderful old-fashioned blooms, she was taking note of the incredible number of breakfast choices on the table.

Having no idea what she would like, Andreo, it seemed, had just ordered up everything for her.

Without warning, her eyes stung with tears and, with a choky little laugh of embarrassment over her own teeming emotions, she dashed away that betraying moisture. Her hand not quite steady, she reached for a fresh roll and buttered it and drank down one of the fruit juices. But it was just no use trying to block out the thoughts pressing in on her: Andreo was, indeed, pretty special. She could not remember when, if ever, any man had made such an effort on her behalf. Her own father had not given two hoots when his own last-minute demands first thing in the morning had ensured that she'd rarely had time to eat before she'd rushed out to work.

'You might as well learn it now,' Martin Stevenson had told her with excruciating bitterness more than once over the years. 'Life's *tough*.'

Cocooned in her warm, happy feelings about Andreo, Pippa went shopping. In fast succession she bought a black trouser suit, comfortable loafers and fresh underwear in the same store that had supplied her entire wardrobe. She really hoped that it wasn't her dress sense that had drawn him because she had never had a flair for choosing clothes or doing her hair or make-up, she conceded ruefully. How superficial in his judgements was a guy who looked as though he had sprung live from a glossy magazine of sophisticated, classy, handsome men? Possibly dating Andreo was likely to demand a lot from her…but since when had she not been up to a challenge?

Chin at an upbeat angle, Pippa entered the Venstar building with a decided smile lurking in her clear blue eyes. In the lift she stood beside two women talking about the employee meeting that was being held on the third floor. The events room that was always used for large staff gatherings was packed. Pippa slipped in at the back just as a middle-aged director lifted a welcoming hand to announce, 'Andreo D'Alessio, Venstar's new president!'

Pippa saw Andreo, *her* Andreo, rise from his seat at the top table. Magnificent in a pale grey business suit worn with a dark blue shirt and toning silk tie, lean, sardonic face grave, he made her heart leap and her tummy fill with butterflies. Trying to keep a silly smile from forming on her lips, she felt quite ridiculously proud and possessive of him. Only when she was about to look away rather than risk other people noticing who she was staring at did it finally dawn on her that *her* Andreo was striding forward to raise a silencing hand in response to the thunderous tide of applause.

For a long, timeless moment, she assumed that he was acting as spokesman for his employer and then the director addressed him as, 'Mr D'Alessio' and all such hope died. Disbelief made her eyes huge and her mouth fall open and, inside her suit jacket, her heart seemed to be running a one-minute mile so noisily that it was interfering with her hearing.

The finance project assistant, Jonelle, shifted closer to speak to her. 'Go on, admit it. For a bloke as hot as Andreo D'Alessio, just about any woman would stretch a point and consider donning diamond-studded handcuffs! I mean, you wouldn't throw him out of bed, would you?'

Pippa tried to laugh off the comment but her voice had vanished and her lips were too slow and clumsy to shape words for her. But then, had she been able to rescue her vocal cords and make sound, she would have sobbed with raging unbelief and pain.

CHAPTER FOUR

SHOCK was rolling over Pippa in a suffocating, chilling tidal wave: *her* Andreo was Venstar's president, the fabulously wealthy Italian entrepreneur and womaniser, Andreo D'Alessio!

Gutted by that revelation and much too devastated to immediately react, Pippa listened dully to Andreo giving a short, witty speech about his plans for Venstar. *Her* Andreo? Since when? Sick with shame and the most terrible sense of hurt and betrayal, she shivered, cold to the very centre of her bones, even her skin clammy. Why had he lied to her? Why had he let her think that he was just another employee? How could he have done that to her? What sort of sick, perverted sense of humour did the guy have?

Only then did she remember that she had made the first error in mistaking the small, portly man at the podium for Venstar's new owner. She had then made critical remarks about Andreo D'Alessio. Was that why he had slept with her? The ultimate put-down? Her tummy gave a nauseous roll. How very funny he must have thought he was being when he'd assured her that Andreo was a very common name in Italy and she'd swallowed his stupid lie whole!

Across the room, Andreo's attention was caught by the apricot glint of her bright head. His recognition of her was instantaneous even though her hair was caught up in a rather juvenile pony-tail and her face was bare of make-up. Having assumed that she would do exactly as he had asked, he was disconcerted. In fact, he frowned. Why the hell hadn't she remained at the hotel? Even as he looked he saw her spin away and almost cannon into a group of people in her haste to leave the room. Of course, he conceded grimly, she would immediately have learned who he was.

Instinct urged Andreo to follow her, but he was determined not to make a parade of their relationship during office hours. He was aware that his blatant pursuit of her the night before had been far from discreet. Annoyance flared in him at that grudging acknowledgement. Philly *should* have listened to him and taken the day off. Why was she so stubborn? Now instead of discovering his identity over a relaxing meal, she was finding it out in rather more challenging circumstances.

'I find it hard to believe that your being late today was accidental,' Cheryl Long was informing Pippa in a sharp tone at that exact same moment. 'I wasn't able to show the Kelvedon project figures to senior management because I had no idea that you had sent the file back to Acquisitions. That caused me a *lot* of embarrassment!'

Staff nearby stiffened at that unjust attack but Pippa was much too devastated over what she had just discovered about Andreo to feel the full bite of Cheryl's outrageous accusation. She said nothing because she would have felt foolish defending herself against such a ridiculous charge.

'I'd like you to use my old desk from now on,' Cheryl added, determined, it seemed, to get a reaction out of her subordinate.

'Fine.' Pippa began to clear out her desk drawers.

Cheryl allowed a small smile to play over her burgundy lips and murmured with studied casualness and in an almost friendly tone, 'Oh, I'll need a copy of the presentation you planned to give at this afternoon's meeting for Mr D'Alessio's benefit.'

'I'm afraid I haven't prepared one,' Pippa replied.

'But you *must* have done...' the brunette asserted, her smile falling away at ludicrous speed.

'No, I hadn't got around to it.' Pippa saw no reason to point out that had she been given the job of manager, she would have devoted all of the previous day to that most important task.

Cheryl gave her a furious look of disbelief and, turning on her heel, she stalked across the room and entered Ricky Brownlow's office with only the smallest warning knock.

'Life around here is going to be hell,' Jonelle forecast gloomily to nobody in particular.

'I never thought she'd be such an unbelievable cow,' someone else whispered aghast. 'I mean, she's always been good for a laugh.'

'I can't understand how on earth she....' Jonelle fell silent, possibly appreciating that such remarks were tactless within Pippa's hearing.

In the uneasy silence, Pippa relocated her possessions to her new desk.

'What did you think of Andreo D'Alessio's girlfriend last night?' one of the other women asked Jonelle with determined cheer.

'The redhead? She was sex on legs. Every bloke in the place was drooling over her to the most disgusting extent,' Jonelle lamented. 'If that's the standard of the competition, what hope have us more ordinary types got with him?'

'None at all, I should think.' The older woman chuckled. 'I got the impression that as couples go those two were rather well matched.'

'Matched? In height, I suppose you mean.' Jonelle pulled an unimpressed face.

'Come on…he could hardly bear to take his eyes off her for longer than twenty seconds. She's got him tagged and good luck to her. Didn't she remind you of anyone?'

'Like who?'

'There was just something very familiar about her. I don't know what it was but I thought that maybe she was a model and I'd seen pictures of her somewhere.' .

'She didn't remind me of anyone,' Jonelle retorted.

Pippa had grown tense, but her tension ebbed as the subject was dropped. Of course, nobody was going to recognise her, she told herself bracingly. She busied herself with work that she herself had given Cheryl the previous week. The task was well beneath her ability and, in failing to engage her brain, ensured that as she emerged from the shock of having discovered Andreo's true identity her angry pain only became more raw at the edges.

Never in her life had she felt more humiliated. Andreo had deceived her with a cruel and heartless masquerade. He had lied to her and betrayed her trust. But what kind of an idiot had she been to trust a guy she had only just met? What she had believed to be a wonderfully special and romantic encounter now seemed much more like a sleazy one-night stand. Hurt distaste filled her. He was a notorious womaniser. How come she hadn't at least recognised that reality?

After all, he had been as sleek and sophisticated as the legendary Casanova. Her soft, full mouth compressed. She had been too naive to recognise Andreo D'Alessio for what he was. But where had her intelligence been? He had handed out orders with the cool authority of a male used to people jumping to do his bidding. Arrogant, confident, forceful in personality. His hotel suite had been very large and opulent. The roses and the expensive array of breakfast choices had been the lavish gestures of a rich man, accustomed to using his wealth to impress a woman. And she *had* been impressed, hadn't she? Without warning, a hot tide of moisture hit the back of Pippa's eyes in a stinging flood.

Getting up from her desk, she headed straight for the cloakroom. There she stared at herself with loathing in the mirror until those weak tears had receded of their own volition. How could she be hurting so much? So the fairy tale had been an illusion. And she was *surprised*? As her late father had often reminded her, life was tough. What she had to do was move herself on and focus on something else. But what? Her lacklustre future with a company that had refused her promotion and moreover suggested she take a lengthy career break? That was when Pippa decided that at the end of her three weeks of leave she would not be returning to work at Venstar.

Instead, she would hand in her notice and make a fresh start elsewhere. Some place where looks did not count more than ability and where hard work and results were rewarded. Some place where she had *not* slept with her boss. Settling her tremulous lips into a firmer line, Pippa steadied herself. That was *his* fault too...that she had betrayed her principles and ended up sleeping with her employer. An amount of anger that left her downright giddy shot through her in a re-energising surge. In retrospect she could not credit Andreo's reckless behaviour and she knew then that she would know no peace until she confronted him.

She took the lift up to the executive floor. It was almost lunch time and the corridors were busy with people hurrying back and forth. She headed straight for the managing director's office, knocked once on the door and entered before anyone could try to prevent her.

Taken aback by that sudden interruption, Andreo swung round from the computer screen and focused on Pippa instead. On a slender woman dressed all in black with eyes as bright and blue as sapphires and a mouth that even unadorned was as inviting as a ripe cherry.

He smiled because he was pleased that she had come to him and then wondered why she was wearing a suit at least a size too large for her.

It was his smile that first threatened Pippa's tenuous self-control. That he could still smile when she felt lacerated was almost more than she could bear. But that smile was also a trip wire for it had megawatt charm and she found herself staring at him, drinking in his lean bronzed features and the stunning impact of the dark golden eyes welded to her. A host of intimate recollections drowned out her anger. Suddenly she was back where she had been the night before, blushing like mad and as overwhelmed by the power of her own frantic response as an adolescent in the presence of her idol.

'Philly…' In one strikingly graceful movement, Andreo rose to his full height and extended his hand.

The name he employed broke her spell. 'It's Pippa, actually, Pippa Stevenson,' she told him in a high, unnatural voice. 'Andreo…how could you have lied to me the way you did?'

Andreo let his hand fall back to his side, keen eyes narrowing, for he did not like her tone. 'I didn't tell you a single lie,' he countered.

'But you knew that I hadn't the smallest suspicion that you were Andreo D'Alessio. If you weren't prepared to tell me the truth, you should've left me alone.'

'But you didn't *want* to be left alone, *cara mia*,'

Andreo traded smooth as polished jet, wondering why she was making such a fuss over news that would delight any normal woman. So, instead of being a nine-to-five worker, he owned the business. So, instead of being reasonably successful, he was a mega achiever. So, instead of earning a good salary, he was filthy rich and in possession of a private jet and an array of luxury homes. What was there to complain about? And where the hell did she think she was coming from when she accused him of lying? He had been careful not to tell her a single untruth.

Tension was pounding out an enervated beat at Pippa's temples but she lifted her head high and she breathed in deep. 'You are my employer and I had a right to know that.'

'*Dio mio*...what a fuss you are making about nothing!' Andreo censured, a satiric dark brow elevated in a manner that would have warned the wary that his patience was running out.

'Nothing?' Pippa gasped, jolted into agonised reaction by his bold refusal to acknowledge the damage he had done.

'Between us and after last night, it *should* mean nothing, *carissima*.' Andreo rephrased as he strode forward to reach for her clenched hands.

Pippa sidestepped him and spread her arms wide in angry condemnation. 'You're even worse than I thought you would be—'

'And what's that supposed to mean?' Andreo demanded.

Pippa kept her eyes wide and fixed in focus because tears were damming up again behind them. Tears of rage and disappointment. He was not the guy she had thought he was. 'I would never have spent the night with you if

I had known I worked for you. Do you make a habit of sleeping with your employees?'

'*Per meraviglia…*' A faint but perceptible rise of blood illuminated his high cheekbones and his tall, powerful length went rigid. Blazing golden eyes seared her in punishment for her daring to ask such a question. 'Never before have I become intimate with a member of my staff!'

'I wish I could say I believed you but it's difficult,' Pippa admitted curtly. 'Particularly when it's obvious to me that you haven't the faintest idea of the boundaries that a decent employer should respect!'

'Your anger I will take, but your insolence I *refuse* to accept,' Andreo murmured in icy warning.

Pippa trembled and her hands knotted into tighter fists. 'You're not even ashamed of yourself, are you?'

Andreo surveyed her steadily. 'Do I have regrets about spending the night with you? No. I had too good a time. I don't consider our relationship a mistake. As far as I'm concerned the fact that I employ you is virtually irrelevant as an issue. I own many different businesses and employ many thousands of workers and my time here at Venstar will be brief. You will neither gain nor lose by my interest.'

'Oh? And how do you make that out?' Distress made Pippa's voice rise half an octave. 'If a colleague was to recognise me as the redhead with you at last night's party, I could never hold my head up again! My only consolation is that I wasn't recognised and that nobody knows what a fool I made of myself!'

Andreo closed lean brown hands over hers in a deliberate move that prevented her from walking away again. He could not imagine how her co-workers could possibly have failed to identify her and he could only believe that she was kidding herself on that score. Enough was enough, he decided in growing frustration. It was time she calmed down and stopped attacking him. 'You didn't make a fool of yourself. That isn't how it was between us. Why are you talking like this? Two people met and succumbed to the same potent attraction—'

'It's not that simple—'

Andreo stared at her with level intensity. 'It *is* if you want it to be, *cara*.'

Painfully aware of the rich, dark pull of his sensual attraction, which was all the more devastating when backed by his powerful personality, Pippa wrenched her hands free of his with positive violence. 'I don't want it to be. You pretended to be someone you weren't. The guy I *thought* you were doesn't exist. I wouldn't have been attracted to a sexist playboy like you in a million years!'

As she attempted to move away Andreo blocked her path and scorching golden eyes assailed hers in a look as aggressive as an assault. 'I think you had better explain that condemnation in language I can be sure I understand.'

Her throat convulsed but she stared back at him in agonised defiance, the sense of loss tearing at her only increasing her bitterness and armouring her with more obstinate determination. 'You cost me my promotion even before you arrived in this building. I heard one of the men who met you in Naples telling a director how unimpressed you were by my picture in the company newsletter and how you preferred sexy, fanciable women in executive posts...'

'That is a complete fallacy.' Pippa Stevenson? Her name had set off a faint familiar bell in Andreo's memory. The company newsletter. He remembered that publication and leafed through the documents on his desk in search of the copy that he had retained.

'I applied for the management position in my section,' Pippa continued unsteadily. 'A job which I had already been doing for some months and which I had every reason to hope would become mine on a permanent basis. Instead the promotion went to another woman, who is not only junior to me in status and unqualified but, also, very much prettier—'

'*Dio mio*...this photo does nothing for you! In this guise even I would be challenged to recognise you,' Andreo confessed with a frown of exasperation. 'But I made only one reference to your appearance that day in Naples. I did not make a single politically incorrect or provocative comment about pretty or sexy women in management, I assure you. I only said that you looked slovenly—'

'I beg your pardon?' Pippa exclaimed in a stricken tone of wonderment.

'And, unfortunately, you *do* look rather untidy in this picture,' Andreo breathed, standing his ground, shooting from the hip in self-defence.

Slovenly? She could not believe he had employed that word as a description of her appearance. Moving forward to snatch the newsletter from him, she gasped, 'What's wrong with me?'

'I shouldn't need to tell you. Look at your hair...it's all over the place.' Andreo found himself studying her while she pored over the newsletter picture and noticed that once again her hair presented, at first glance at least, a rather mussed appearance. Tiny cinnamon curls clustered at her hairline and a rebellious wave was threatening to ruin the once-smooth fall of the silky strands on top of her head. Far from being straight, he registered, her hair seemed to be exuberantly curly.

'Slovenly...' Pippa repeated sickly.

Andreo found that that hurt intonation hit him like a four-car pile-up but he was bone-deep stubborn and as angry with her as any male wholly unaccustomed to female censure could be. 'There's a button missing from your jacket and the trousers look like you slept in them. You don't look very smart. That's *all* I said.'

Painful colour had drenched her cheeks. She bit down hard on the soft underside of her lower lip and tasted blood. That photo had been taken barely a week after her father's death and she had rushed into the room, all breathless and apologetic and the last to join the line-up. It was an old trouser suit and she could see that it was not flattering. But that word, 'slovenly', mortified her and she was appalled that he could be so cruelly inconsiderate of her feelings.

'That is the sole remark that I made,' Andreo asserted, deciding just then that he would never, ever again comment on an employee's personal appearance without very serious forethought.

Whatever, he had cost her the job of Finance Manager even though he was refusing to acknowledge it, Pippa reflected unhappily. He had to know just how eager the Venstar executives were to please him. His criticism would have been sufficient to put a large question mark over the advisability of raising her to managerial status.

'I want to repeat that I passed no inappropriate comments relating to my supposed physical preferences in female employees,' Andreo completed with sardonic clarity.

Pippa remained mutinously silent. He might have what it took to pull women in a very big way, but he was also very much one of the guys: earthly male, athletic, dazzlingly confident, popular with his own sex. A male-dominated culture operated at executive level within Venstar. If Andreo *had* chosen to make Jack-the-lad jokes about women at that session in Naples, she was well aware that he could not have chosen a more receptive audience.

'I *assume* that you accept that,' Andreo prompted with speaking emphasis.

A laugh that was no laugh at all fell from her lips. 'I don't know if I do. Your behaviour last night made it clear that you don't consider yourself bound by the standards that the average employer would automatically respect.'

Andreo threw up his arrogant dark head. 'I don't accept that contention.'

'Why should you when you're so convinced that no rules whatsoever should apply to you?' Pippa shot at him with a fierce, tremulous edge of accusation to her voice. 'You seem to believe that you have a God-given right to do exactly as you please regardless of how it might affect others. What about my rights? You're my boss and, had I known that, what happened between us would never have happened. I wouldn't have dreamt of making an exhibition of myself with you in front of the people I have to work with either!'

'*Dio mio*, what is done is done...' Andreo entrapped and held the distressed blue of her gaze with smouldering golden eyes.

'It should never have happened,' Pippa mumbled chokily, striving with all her might to disconnect from the heated charge of his magnetic appraisal. 'And slovenly means grubby...and I have never been less than clean in my whole life—'

'I never said that you were…just a little untidy. I was not aware that the word had any other connotation.' Andreo could not credit the effort he was making to placate her. He was annoyed with her. He had every reason to be annoyed with her but he still found himself closing his arms round the general space she occupied as slowly and sneakily as if he were about to try and hug dynamite.

'I am *not* untidy…what are you doing?' It shook Pippa that even in the wake of all her proud words of rejection little miniature fireworks of wild anticipation started fizzing low in her tummy the minute he put his arms round her.

'Tell me you don't want this,' Andreo growled sexily.

Her body was all hot and quivery and eager and shamed colour warmed her cheeks at that awareness. Her breasts felt heavy and tender, the straining peaks tautening into hard little points of betrayal below her jacket. 'Stop looking at me like that,' she pleaded.

With a husky laugh, Andreo bent his handsome dark head and teased her soft lips open with shattering carnal expertise. 'We need to talk. We could have lunch instead of dinner, *cara*—'

'No…'

'Dinner is such a long way away…why should we be that patient?' Andreo's breath fanned her cheek as he came back for a more intimate sortie, letting his tongue delve an erotic path between her lips and making her vent an involuntary moan.

'Back off…my career and my reputation are important to me and this is a mug's game,' Pippa muttered shakily, desperate for another kiss but fighting the lure of him with all her might, knowing all too well just how much she was likely to hate herself if she let him come between her and her wits a second time.

She could smell the evocative male scent of his skin, awesomely familiar to her, shockingly exciting. She felt dizzy and emotional and she wanted to throw herself the last six inches that separated them. She could feel him willing her to do it too. He had an attitude problem. She knew that now. A big backlog of her misguided predecessors had flattered his ego and taught him that he could talk and laugh and seduce his way out of awkward moments. He was manipulative, utterly without conscience, ruthless enough to go to any length to win. He was *not* Mr Wonderful, Mr Perfect, that one very special guy she had believed he was.

But even though she knew all that, resisting Andreo was tearing her apart at the seams. He had taught her to want him and she had been bitten deep by her own yearning. She felt achingly vulnerable and furious with herself for not having sufficient will-power to put him in his place.

'*Amore*…let's not make heavy weather of this,' Andreo drawled, his glorious Italian accent skimming down her sensitive backbone and just tying her up in pathetic shivering knots of responsiveness. 'In your heart, you know very well that you're going to forgive me for all my supposed sins.'

Fury with him and her own weakness made the tears she had held back for well over an hour surge free in a dismaying flood. Without thinking, she wiped her eyes with the back of her hand and dislodged one of her contact lenses. 'Oh, no!' she groaned and dropped down onto her knees. 'Don't move…I've lost a lens!'

Andreo dropped down into an athletic crouch and picked up the tiny lens from the polished wood floor. 'I have it,' he murmured, removing a sheet of paper from the desk and folding the lens into the pocket he had fashioned for it. 'So you wear contacts...'

Pippa wondered if he had ever made a pass at a woman who wore spectacles before and then sucked in a stark breath of despair, wishing that she had the power to regain control of her own brain. 'I'm not about to forgive you,' she stated between gritted teeth. 'I don't want to see you again. I just want to forget that last night happened—'

'Go ahead...we can have a hell of a time rediscovering the joys and reliving the highlights tonight, *bella mia*.'

'Why won't you listen to what I'm saying?' Pippa demanded in fierce frustration, still down on her knees as she tucked the folded paper into her jacket.

'Whether you knew it or not, you signed up for more than one night when you shared my bed.' Andreo rested brilliant dark golden eyes on her in challenge. 'I still want you. You still want me. While I can't understand how your colleagues could have failed to recognise you at the hotel last night, I'm willing to be discreet if that's what you prefer—'

'Stop trying to tempt me,' Pippa cut in a fierce accusing tone even while she leant almost imperceptibly closer to him. 'I wouldn't waste ten minutes of my time on a guy who gives women sex toys for his amusement!'

His black brows drew together, lashes dropping low over his amazing eyes. He gave her a slashing grin that made her want to hit him and pin him horizontal to the floor at one and the same time. '*Sex*...toys?'

'The diamond-studded handcuffs...I read about them in a newspaper,' she informed him thinly.

'Shame on you, *cara mia*. You've been reading real trash,' Andreo murmured in unembarrassed silken reproof. 'And I hate to be the one to disappoint you but you're about as ready for sex toys as I am for celibacy!'

Vaulting upright, he stretched down a hand to help her up too. But in almost the same moment Pippa heard the door open and a male voice address Andreo in his own language. She almost died on the spot and shot right under his desk to curl up into a remarkably small ball.

Sal Rissone made a praiseworthy effort not to let his attention touch on the woman hiding under Andreo's trendy glass desk.

'Just pretend that she's as invisible as she thinks she is,' Andreo told him in Italian.

'Am I allowed to ask what she's doing there?' his childhood friend enquired, deadpan.

'Protecting herself from the embarrassment of being seen in my office. She…she gets hyper about crazy things,' Andreo murmured almost defensively, shrugging a broad shoulder. 'She's a sensitive woman.'

Sixth sense warned Sal not to crack the rather coarse joke brimming on his lips. Self-evidently, Andreo had decided that hyper was cute and sensitive and worthy of respect. Andreo, who thought women were interchangeable commodities pretty much put on earth for his sole enjoyment, was making excuses for one so off-the-wall she was hiding under his desk. Andreo, who had such very pronounced ideas of what he liked and what he disliked. Sal could not wait to call his wife and share the news that Andreo was acting as strangely today as he had the night before.

Seconds after the door closed on Sal's departure, Pippa shot out from her hiding place. Standing up, she smoothed herself down with shaking hands while refusing to award Andreo a single glance and walked straight back out of his office again. After all, what more was there to say? She had made her feelings clear. Furthermore, she was all too painfully conscious that she had a very low resistance threshold to those sleek, dark, gorgeous good looks of his.

Mid-afternoon, instead of working, she found herself staring into space, utterly, frighteningly shorn of her usual great concentration. She tried to boot Andreo back out of her thoughts but he hung in there as if he were tattooed on her brain cells. She was furious with herself. He had no shame. He would not agree that he had been an irresponsible, selfish toad in refusing to admit that he was her boss. So now she knew what the surprise he had been planning to break to her over dinner would have been...

Yes, now she knew and she also had the unarguable proof of how basically unimportant he had deemed the whole issue to be. Brow furrowing, she reconsidered that angle as she recalled his insistence that the attraction between them should take priority over all else. Hadn't he also sworn that she was the only employee he had ever been involved with? Taken together with his behaviour, didn't those facts suggest that Andreo might be genuinely interested in her? For goodness' sake, was she already falling back into that demeaning trap of dreaming that her wildest fantasies could come true?

How naive could a woman be? Andreo D'Alessio was a rat! A sleek smooth rat. He was also very, very rich and he had a very bad reputation with women. How likely was it that such a male had even vaguely decent intentions towards the stupid, trusting virgin who had flung herself into his bed the very first time they'd met? Pippa paled. She was ashamed of her own desperate desire to believe that she could trust him. Hadn't she learned anything at all since she was seventeen?

That last summer in France she had fallen in love for the first time. A student staying in the neighbouring village, Pete, had been four years older, blond, good-looking, a motorbike fanatic. For a whole month, she and Hilary and occasionally even Jen had hung out with Pete and his mates. Tabby had met the boys too, but once her friend had met Christien, who was now her husband, Tabby had spent all her time with him.

Pippa had fallen like a ton of bricks for Pete. He had held hands with her, kissed her, acted as though he was interested in her and her life. Perhaps she ought to have questioned why he'd been so keen to encourage her to talk about how worried she'd been about Tabby, who had embarked on a wild affair with Christien. Tabby with her caramel-blonde hair and voluptuous figure had always attracted the guys and she had come out with them all again only because Christien had been away on business.

That day, Pete had taken Tabby on the back of his bike instead of Pippa. Although he had pretty much ignored Pippa, she had honestly thought he was just being friendly. So when he had kissed Tabby right in front of her, she had been shattered, but pride had made her hide her pain. Tabby had had no idea that Pippa had regarded Pete as her boyfriend and she had said afterwards, 'I was annoyed when Pete came on to me but he told me he'd been waiting his chance with me all summer and I felt really sorry for the poor bloke…because, let's face it, the only bloke in the world for me is Christien.'

The hardest thing that Pippa had ever done was pretend indifference to the humiliation that Pete had inflicted on her. Pete had just used her to pump her for information about Tabby and as an excuse to call at the farmhouse where they'd all been staying in the undoubted hope of running into her friend again. What little faith Pippa had

had in her own judgement of the opposite sex had taken a hammering, for Pete had made it painfully obvious that he'd felt absolutely nothing for her.

Surfacing from those wounding recollections, Pippa looked up with a dazed aspect to her bespectacled blue eyes when she saw the post boy poised in front of her desk holding a gigantic basket of flowers.

'Wow...' Jonelle gushed with inquisitive eyes. 'Is it your birthday or something?'

Gulping, Pippa scrambled upright. She detached the envelope from the basket handle and tore into it with hands that she could not keep steady.

'Text me your address...finish early?'

There was no signature and it was not his handwriting but she knew the glorious arrangement was from him because she did not know another living soul in the country who could have afforded to spend that much on flowers. Her knees felt wobbly and she dropped back into her seat. She decided that it would be more dignified to ignore both the gesture and the message, but she was horribly conscious of just how badly she wanted to dig out her mobile phone and text him. She had never had a guy to do that with.

'Call for you, Pippa...' Jonelle announced, having answered the extension on what was now Cheryl's desk.

Pippa took the call.

'Do we have to sneak around?' Andreo complained huskily. 'My English grandmother used to say, "Tell the truth and shame the devil".'

'It's a pity her outlook didn't rub off on you!' Pippa whispered in a controlled hiss while she slid her forefinger into the long ringlet that had broken loose from her pony-tail and wound bright strands of hair round and round in a frantic, enervated spiral.

'I had to throw all my staff out of the boardroom to call you—'

'Did I ask you to?' But an appreciative grin tugged at Pippa's mouth.

'I need to use *my* phone!' Without any further warning, Cheryl simply snatched the receiver from Pippa's hold and stabbed a punitive finger down on the cut-off button.

In astonishment, Pippa wheeled round. 'There was no reason to do that—'

'Wasn't there?' Cheryl gave her an enraged scrutiny. 'Thanks to you I've just gone through the worst ordeal of my life!'

'Sorry?' Pippa was now noticing how hot, bothered and tearful the pretty brunette looked.

'I gave my presentation and that sarcastic bastard, D'Alessio, blew me away with the most awful questions. I couldn't answer them and he treated me like I was stupid…it's your fault that I wasn't well enough prepared!' Cheryl was sobbing in noisy earnest long before she reached the end of that impassioned outburst.

In the ghastly silence that stretched through the section, Ricky Brownlow hastened up, his discomfiture in the radius of Cheryl's distress palpable. 'Miss Long's upset and she doesn't know what she's saying. Pippa… er…I'm sorry about this. I'm sure Cheryl will want to apologise to you later when she's feeling more herself.'

As the blond man urged the crying brunette into his office, Cheryl was heard to loudly deny any desire to apologise to Pippa for *anything*.

'Since when did Ricky get so chummy with Cheryl?' someone asked.

'Seems she found out the hard way that she couldn't

do Pippa's job. Serves her right too.' Jonelle sniffed. 'I'm more amazed she had the nerve to even apply for it!'

Pippa's mobile phone buzzed. Instead of answering it, she switched it off. It would be Andreo and she did not trust herself to check that it was and still ignore his call. Stuffing her phone back into her bag, she went back to work. As she was leaving an hour later Cheryl sidled up to her, her eyes and her nose still pink, her resentment barely concealed as she forced out grudging words of apology for her verbal attack.

Pippa was as gracious as she felt she could be but the brunette's behaviour had merely underlined her own conviction that her own days of working at Venstar were strictly numbered. When she got home to the terraced house that she had once shared with her late father, she phoned out for a pizza. She loosed her wayward hair, finger-combed her curls and shed her suit in favour of a T-shirt and shorts. Making herself comfortable, she rang Tabby at her Breton home and asked if she could come and stay with her friend and her husband for a while.

'I can't believe you're finally taking a holiday and coming over to see us!' After the ghastly day at work that Pippa had endured, Tabby's bubbling delight warmed her.

Following that call, Pippa studied her familiar surroundings and finally conceded that she was bored and dissatisfied with her dull existence. She decided that that was most probably why she had gone off the rails with Andreo D'Alessio and ditched her principles. Alcohol had played its unfortunate part too, she told herself grimly. It was not that *he* was so impossibly attractive, but more that he had caught her in a weak moment.

Just for once she had longed to do something different, something adventurous, something that wasn't sensible.

Everything else in her life was certainly sensible. Right
down to her very wardrobe and rarely varied routine. Her
grandparents and her parents had been comfortably off
and, thanks to their canny financial planning, she owned
her home outright, enjoyed a healthy savings account and
could afford to take her time about job hunting. In twelve
days' time, she would be in Brittany. While she was over
there, shouldn't she explore the possibility of living and
working in France for a while?

No sooner had that idea occurred to Pippa than her
thoughts leapt ahead of her. She was free to do as she
liked and rather than burn all her boats at once and risk
selling her terraced home, she could let it out to tenants
instead. Her late mother had been French and Pippa had
grown up bilingual. All things considered, launching a
fresh phase of her life across the English Channel would
not be quite as risky for her as it would be for others,
she decided.

Her front doorbell buzzed. Her mouth watering at the
prospect of a slice of pizza, she answered it and then fell
back a step in surprise and confusion.

Andreo took advantage of her disarray to push the door
back and stride into the hall. Tall, broad-shouldered and
lean-hipped, his proud dark head at an angle, he rested
brilliant golden eyes with speaking satisfaction on the
basket of flowers that she had carted back from the office
and then he switched his bright gaze to her.

'You aren't dressed yet, *cara*,' he commented in his
lazy drawl.

'I'm not d-dressed because I'm not going anywhere.'
At the nervous stammer of her own voice, flames of pink
burnished Pippa's delicate cheekbones. 'And I've already
told you that…why are you so persistent?'

CHAPTER FIVE

ANDREO almost laughed out loud. In asking him that question, could Pippa be serious?

Sexual desire was like a juggernaut inside him, driving him back to her with relentless force and determination. Lean dark face taut, he raked his incisive gaze slowly and carefully over her. He had to admit that she was a far cry from the sultry beauties he usually took to his bed, women who devoted much of their day to the maintenance of a groomed and flawless appearance. Her cinnamon mop of explosive curls was tousled and curiously appealing to him. She wore not a scrap of make-up and she was barefoot. Not even her nails were painted. Her T-shirt and shorts were not of the designer variety either.

But her candid eyes were bright as sapphires against her flushed skin and her soft pink mouth was vulnerable and full. Well washed and faded, the T-shirt moulded her supple curves and delineated pouting breasts rounded as apples and crowned with stiff little nipples.

His all-male body responding with fierce enthusiasm to that provocative evidence that his preoccupation in her was wonderfully matched by hers in him, Andreo murmured thickly, 'I want you too, *bella mia.*'

The whole time that Andreo had been engaged in looking her over with the arrogant assurance of a male well aware of his own breathtaking magnetic attraction, Pippa had found herself welded to the spot with her heartbeat accelerating, her mouth bone-dry and her breath coming in jagged little bursts.

Clad in designer casuals of faultless sophistication, he looked incredibly handsome: cropped black hair glinting below the downlighters, level brows accentuating the masculine perfection of his hard cheekbones and the blue-black shading of his bronzed skin where it roughened in true masculine style round his aggressive jawline. She could literally *feel* his stunning eyes on her and the intensity of his appraisal fired a charge of helpless quivering excitement inside her. Her spine was in a rigid curve, slim shoulders thrown back, an attitude she only then appreciated pushed her braless breasts into prominence. The tingling of her sensitive flesh made her gaze lower and a hot wave of scarlet washed her cheeks when she realised why he was staring at her: the shameless distension of her nipples was obvious even through the cotton of her top.

'I don't want you...' she gasped in belated denial, lifting one hand in a blind betraying gesture to steady herself against the wall behind her.

Andreo was incensed with her. 'All I want right now is food—'

'Liar!' Pippa proclaimed.

Andreo sent her a smouldering appraisal, dense black lashes low over burning gold. 'It is polite to make a civilised pretence of patience, *cara mia*.'

Civilised? Since when had he been civilised? Even the alcohol in her bloodstream the night before had not dimmed her awareness of his powerful personality and emphatic individuality. Staring back at him, for all her spoken defiance entrapped by the sheer impact of his exotic dark good looks and sexual vibrancy that close, Pippa shivered. 'Don't pretend with me.'

He quirked a sardonic brow. 'You need me to tell you that, since early this morning, I've been on fire with a very powerful urge to carry you back to bed and sate my every fantasy?'

'I'm not the kind of woman whom men have fantasies about,' Pippa told him with a stony disdain edged with a raw, angry regret that she fought to keep to herself. For at that very moment she longed to be the sort of female who *did* inspire men with such fervour and admiration.

'I only know what you do for me and what we found last night *was*—'

'Just sex.' Pippa thrust up her chin as she forced herself to make that blunt interruption, determined as she was to ensure that he received no opportunity to turn her foolish head again with false flattery. 'That's all it was.'

Andreo was outraged. Times without number he had slept with women and thought in exactly those terms, but no woman had ever treated him to a similar description. He felt insulted beyond relief and furious with her. '*Dio mio*. Why so coarse?' he demanded with seething bite. 'Together we discovered something exceptional. You were a virgin—'

Pippa paled with anger at that embarrassing reminder of the lack of experience that had evidently encouraged his reluctance to accept that she could know what she was talking about when she rejected him. 'Do you have to drag that up?'

'It is relevant. You *chose* me as your first lover,' Andreo reminded her, infuriated by her efforts to brush him off as though he had been some tasteless and misjudged one-night stand.

Her oval face flushed a hot and mortified pink.

Andreo was quick to press his advantage. 'I was concerned then that you would have regrets but don't let that come between us now, *amore*.'

'My choosing you as my first lover meant nothing…nothing at all,' Pippa disclaimed with lacerated pride.

Andreo learned that he could travel from rage to a torn sense of tenderness that threatened to gut him and he loathed the revelation. He knew by her unhappy eyes that she was lying to him but he could not work out why. 'Then why look at me the way you do?'

Pippa went rigid. 'What way?'

A very male smile slashed his lean, strong face. 'I need to draw pictures?'

Temper leapt through her in an energising roar. 'Perhaps you do.'

His molten golden gaze snared hers and her heart crashed against her breastbone as though someone had thrown a panic switch deep down inside her. 'Even the way you look at me speaks to me of your hunger for me…'

'It's only sexual attraction, nothing I can't bury again any time I want to!' Pippa stabbed back in fearful retaliation.

'So…bury me,' Andreo invited in husky challenge, angling down his proud dark head and claiming her full parted lips, prying straight between them with the erotic immediacy of an expert.

For a split second she remained stiff as a coat-hanger and then she trembled violently, shifted forward in a clumsy movement and let her hands close in a feverish embrace over his wide shoulders to steady legs that she could no longer depend on. She moaned as he used his tongue to probe the sensitive reaches of her mouth. The ticklish throb of her tender breasts made her instinctively press into the tough, muscular wall of his hard, masculine body. Fierce sensual excitement currented through her slim body and the intimate ache between her thighs intensified.

Andreo snatched his head up and drew in a stark lungful of air, a suppressed shudder racking his lean, powerful length, a raw Italian curse almost impelled from him by the disciplinary demands of restraining the force of his hunger for her. Shimmering golden eyes locked to her hectically flushed face and swollen mouth. 'You were saying…?' he prompted lethally, hoping like hell that she was a good loser so that he could triumph twice over and just haul her off to the nearest bed.

'Saying?' The word meant nothing to her for Pippa was not thinking just then. Her pale slender fingers stretched up and speared into his luxuriant black hair to yank him back down to her again. 'Kiss,' she told him, all of a quiver against him, hot and restive and in need, all her powers of concentration bent on the single-minded, necessary goal of dragging him back into her arms.

Andreo murmured something husky in Italian and gazed down at her with sizzling satisfaction, glorying in his sensual power over her, neatly choosing to overlook that he had been cursing hers over him just seconds earlier.

'Please…' she framed in uneasy bewilderment, brow indenting, for she had been unlocked from the erotic lure of him long enough by that stage for rational thought to be threatening a return. As the phone began ringing she winced, for she felt as if the slightest external annoyance might tip her over the edge and make her scream or break down.

'You're on a sensual high…coming down hurts, *amore*,' Andreo breathed as he recognised the source of the bemused tears in her eyes.

Shock shrilled through her. It had not occurred to her that the fever pitch of desire that he could rouse her to so easily had another side to the coin: the torment of unsated hunger. Suddenly limp, she rested against him, devastated by her own capacity for passion. He had been in her life barely twenty-four hours and already he had turned it and her upside down with feelings and sensations that she had never dreamt she might fall victim to. It was truly terrifying.

Andreo smoothed a hand over her down-bent head in a soothing gesture. An answering machine clicked on and a man's deep pitched voice broke the humming silence in French.

'Pippa? It's Christien. I need a private word with you…'

Her head came up in surprise and she pulled back from Andreo. The speaker was Tabby's husband. As he was not in the habit of making personal calls to her, Pippa was afraid that something had happened to Tabby and concern sent her flying to the phone. 'Christien?'

But, cool and calm as was his wont, Christien informed her that he was willing to come over to London on the day she wanted to travel and bring her back to France with him that same evening if she would accompany him on a maternity shopping trip on Tabby's behalf. Her lively friend had her own quirky dress sense and Christien might be the living image of the Parisian's legendary sophistication, but he had never yet managed to buy his adoring wife anything to wear that she actually liked.

'Tabby's pregnant again? My goodness…' Pippa had to struggle to keep the dismayed disapproval out of her voice. After all, if her friend was soon to give birth to a *third* child at the tender age of twenty-three years, it was hardly Pippa's place to comment. However, she was seriously tempted to ask Christien if an annual baby was a perquisite of Tabby having married into the top drawer of French society to which he belonged. Surely her poor besotted friend could only be expecting yet again because a mini football team of kids was what Christien's unquenchable masculine ego demanded? Tabby might be blissfully happy with Christien but Pippa put that down to Tabby's loving nature.

'I'll let her tell you all about it herself,' Christien countered finally to bridge the awkward silence that had fallen. 'You're very quiet. Does a shopping trip in my sole company promise to be more than you can stand?'

Beneath Andreo's steady appraisal, Pippa turned a guilty brick-red. Christien had seduced Tabby as a teenager and broken her heart. Their past misunderstandings had been resolved before their marriage a couple of years back but Pippa had never really warmed to her friend's husband. That Christien himself should have guessed that fact, however, mortified her. 'Don't be silly. Your wife's my friend, for goodness' sake—'

'Just tell yourself that you're doing it for Tabby's benefit.' Christien's cool, condescending amusement rarely failed to set Pippa's teeth on edge. 'Don't worry. I've never considered your hostility as an issue personal to me...I know you dislike men.'

At that declaration, Pippa's eyes almost shot out on stalks and she sped into the kitchen to gain the privacy to hiss, 'Is that what you think? Well, let me disabuse you of the suspicion that I'm either gay or a man hater—'

'I wasn't aware—' Christien sounded startled and well he might have done, for when he had brought his wife over to London in recent years Pippa had always been very quiet in his presence.

'In fact right now I'm involved in a passionate affair with an Italian guy!' Pippa asserted in defiant retaliation, hurt and offended by what he had said and desperate to disprove it.

At that rather shattering announcement, Christien just laughed out loud, smoothly assured her that she had mis-understood his meaning but that he was delighted to hear that her private life was flourishing. As she walked back into the hall, mentally kicking herself for rising to Christien's provocative bait, Tabby's husband arranged to pick her up on the relevant date. Wondering if her embarrassment over her wild outburst would have sub-sided even partially by then, she cast aside the cordless phone.

Out in the hall, Andreo had heard most of that exchange. Initially he had only been surprised that Pippa could speak French with the speed and verbal virtuosity of a native but his mood had soon turned dark and stormy. Who the hell was the French guy she was chat-tering to? Why on earth had she looked *so* guilty? Evidently this Christien character was married to her friend yet she had seemed most unhappy to learn that her friend was pregnant again. Weren't women usually over-joyed by that sort of news? Why had she gone into the kitchen to continue the dialogue in urgent secretive whis-pers? Her discomfiture at the risk of being overheard had been pronounced.

Was she in love with her friend's husband? It struck Andreo as a quite likely scenario. In love with a married man and fighting it or in love and flirting like mad with the misbehaving bastard but idealistically resisting temp-tation and refusing to let the relationship become sexual? Was that why she had thrown her virginity away on a total stranger? In a bout of rebellious frustration over the male she could *not* have? *Dio mio*, even worse, Andreo reflected with bitter anger flaming through him like a burning arrow of provocation, had he, Andreo D'Alessio, been only a sexual substitute for some other man? Might that not explain why in the aftermath Pippa should be so very determined to try to deny and indeed forget their intimacy?

Her heart rate picking up speed, her throat dry, Pippa focused on Andreo's lean, dark, devastating profile. She remembered begging for that beautiful, tormenting mouth of his. It had taken him only moments to reduce her to the level of a wanton again. She made herself recall how she had clung and sobbed in the frantic clutches of the sweet agony of ecstasy he had given her the night before and her palms grew damp and her face burned hot as the heart of a fire. All of a sudden she knew why she had hurled that crazy lie at Tabby's husband. Why had she said she was having a passionate affair with an Italian? Her subconscious mind had spoken out loud what she did not have the courage to admit even to herself: she *wanted* to have that affair with Andreo!

'Is there someone else in your life?' Andreo demanded with shocking abruptness.

Taken aback, Pippa breathed, 'Why are you asking me that?'

Andreo settled veiled dark eyes on hers and the strangest little frisson of incipient threat feathered down her taut spinal cord. 'Is there someone?'

'No…of course there isn't…I don't even know why you would ask me again,' she muttered, almost smiling at the realisation that he saw her as rather more irresistible than she saw herself.

Andreo's lean brown fingers clenched into a fist and thrust into the pocket of his well-cut chinos. After what he had overheard, she had to be lying to him. Yet she looked so innocent! He gazed steadily back at her until she had the grace to blush and drop her head. It infuriated him that he should still be as hungry as hell to feel her slim white body under his again.

Pippa tried to be really brave. 'I'm...I'm very drawn to you...'

Andreo shrugged a powerful shoulder, stubborn jawline at a punitive angle, eyes bright with hard gold challenge. 'You said it was just sex, *amore*. That's good enough for me.'

Pippa paled. It wasn't good enough for her. She wanted more. She wanted an open ticket, a proper relationship, the chance of a future with him? Maybe even wedding bells? Did dinosaurs still walk the earth? Or had he stolen her every brain cell? Furious with him for forcing her to face how deep his hold on her already went, she pulled open her front door. 'You're my boss. Let's leave it at that,' she told him woodenly.

Dark fury claimed Andreo for a long, timeless moment. She blew hot, she blew cold. How dared she do that to him? How dared she try to play him at his own game? In that instant, in proud, angry denial of his own fierce, flaring reaction to yet another rejection from her, Andreo was tempted to snatch her up into his arms and carry her into the bedroom and put the 'you're my boss' embargo to the ultimate test. It was his belief that she would crumble. She was *his* woman. Didn't she know that? His every aggressive instinct assured him that he could prove that to her. As soon as he got the chance, however, he intended to check out the identity of the married French guy.

When Andreo had gone, Pippa slumped. She felt horribly let down. Somehow she had lost the plot, for the instant she'd advanced he had seemed to change tack and cool off instead of responding to her greater honesty. Now she could only feel embarrassed that she had harboured naive girlish dreams about a male whose interest in her was unashamedly sexual. She had heard some women say that it was perfectly possible to enjoy sleeping with a guy without emotion getting involved. But she had only shared a bed with Andreo once and already her emotions were in absolute turmoil and he seemed to be occupying her every waking thought. There was a lesson to be learned there, she reflected unhappily.

'I need time to bone up on the latest projects.' The following morning, Cheryl angled a bright, determined smile at Pippa. 'You'll have to stand in for me at today's meeting.'

Secure in the knowledge that she had no intention of remaining at Venstar, Pippa was able to tolerate Cheryl's barefaced cheek in demanding that she take her place in the hot seat.

Ricky Brownlow accompanied Pippa into the lift, clearing his throat to say, 'The directors asked for you specifically. Miss Long was nervous yesterday and Mr D'Alessio became quite impatient with her.'

In the act of wondering why Ricky now seemed to take it upon himself to make excuses for Cheryl, Pippa drew in a short sharp breath at the more challenging news that Andreo would be present at the meeting.

She saw him the minute she entered the room. He looked spectacular and she found it almost impossible to drag her eyes from his lean, powerful face. In a navy business suit, silver-grey shirt and silk tie, he stood more than half a head taller than the men around him. The high heels she had selected from the back of her wardrobe that

morning clicked on the polished wood floor. He swung
round and watched her progress towards the circular conference table: a tall, slender woman with a tumbling mane
of cinnamon curls and blue eyes concealed behind large
spectacles with dark frames that only accentuated the del-
icacy of her fine bone structure and the purity of her skin.

For a split second, when Andreo studied her without
any hint of familiarity, Pippa believed she was about to
succumb to an attack of stage fright, and then a director
voiced an enquiry, helpfully prompting her into her usual
working efficiency. She delivered a detailed breakdown
of the figures that had caused Cheryl such grief a day
earlier. Nobody was left in any doubt that she knew her
field inside out and backwards.

On that same score, Andreo suffered a rare attack of
conscience for he could not disprove Pippa's belief that
his criticism of her appearance had led to the promotion
of an unsuitable candidate over her head. Yet he could
barely credit that a single censorious comment from him
could be responsible for the downright stupid decision to
appoint Cheryl Long to a position for which she was
demonstrably unfit.

As silence fell in the wake of the question-and-answer
session Pippa studied Andreo, wanting him to look at her,
needing him to notice her, shaken by how fierce that
craving was. His intent dark golden scrutiny rested on
her for only the briefest moment. But for Pippa, while
that moment lasted it was as though their companions
just faded out from her awareness. Butterflies broke loose
in her tummy and an irresistible urge to smile almost
overcame her self-discipline.

'You have an exceptional grasp of financial planning,'
Andreo acknowledged with approval.

An unearthly silence fell round the table.

At the compliment, Pippa turned pink with pleasure. Andreo sprang upright and shifted a lean staying hand in an indication that he would like her to remain behind. Almost unbearably conscious of the veiled curiosity of her companions, she hovered until he finally turned back to her. 'I'd like to discuss your future with Venstar over dinner this evening. We'll go straight from the office and eat early...if that suits you?'

'Er...yes, of course,' Pippa muttered hastily, wondering under what terms she was being invited. Strictly business as she herself had requested? She could not fault his present attitude to her. His attention had not lingered on her once and now, in receipt of her agreement, he swung away to deal with someone else. He was driving her out of her mind, she conceded wretchedly. He was behaving like her boss and she couldn't bear it! Yet wasn't that how she had asked him to behave? But she couldn't handle being treated as though she were merely another anonymous employee. She felt absolutely gutted when he no longer looked or smiled at her.

'You want me too...' Andreo had told her and he had been much more on target than she had been prepared to admit. Was she guilty of being a closet romantic who needed to dress up sex with more lasting feelings? For a deeper relationship was not on offer, was it? How could it be? Andreo had been upfront about the fact that his time at Venstar would be brief. He wanted to go to bed with her again. He had been outstandingly frank on that score and why should he not have been? He *was* a notorious womaniser and the last guy alive on whom a sane woman would focus romantic expectations. Why couldn't she meet him on the same ground and accept that all she would ever share with Andreo would be a physical relationship? In ten days she would be packing to leave

London for France and embarking on a new phase of her life. Why didn't she just reach out and take what she wanted for the next week and a half?

An affair limited by time boundaries that would ensure that she did not get too involved and as a result…hurt. An affair on *her* terms. She would be in control. It wouldn't, it couldn't get messy within the space of a few days. In such a truncated time frame there was surely no room for complications or pain. Her chin came up, eyes alight with hope and pure bubbling happiness. She could have him for a little while, enjoy him the way one enjoyed luxurious chocolates and then go back on a normal healthy and sensible diet.

'U were right. I want u 2,' she texted Andreo before she could lose her nerve.

Travelling in his limo across the city Andreo read that message with pleated dark brows and wondered why she had changed her mind. Had his suspicion that she was hooked on her friend's husband been way off target? It seemed it might well have been and he winced, wondering why he had been so unusually fanciful. Undoubtedly there was a more reasonable explanation than that which had appealed to his more cynical streak. Was he becoming overly distrustful of women? Almost simultaneously, the grim mood that had settled over Andreo and that he had refused to acknowledge evaporated. He pictured Pippa as she had looked in the conference room that morning: sunshine firing her vibrant hair, eyes bright as gemstones against her fine porcelain skin. Even the most fleeting thought of her stirred a dulled ache of arousal in his groin.

'Wise woman. C u l8r,' he responded by text.

His PA called Pippa to tell her what time she would be picked up at the rear entrance. The afternoon drifted past Pippa while she lost herself in a daydream. By the time she emerged from the building, having spent an inordinate amount of time fussing with her hair, she was on a nervous high of anticipation. A chauffeur swung out of the long silver limousine waiting by the kerb and opened the passenger door for her. Endeavouring to act as though limos were two a penny in her world, she climbed in.

Andreo surveyed her with burnished golden eyes framed by black spiky lashes. He looked incredibly handsome and her heart raced so fast she felt giddy and breathless.

'So now you're mine on request, *bella mia*...' he breathed, savouring the syllables in the most impossibly sexy style.

As he urged her into connection with his big powerful frame, she blushed at the reality that she could barely wait for him to touch her. He meshed one long-fingered hand into her bright hair and claimed her lips with hungry, driven urgency. She shivered and pushed up against him, temporarily so bereft of anything but her own overwhelming need to connect with him again that the move was instinctive.

'We have business to discuss,' Andreo groaned, drawing back from her.

'What sort of business?'

But the limo had come to a halt and the dialogue was shelved until they were seated at a corner table in a fashionable restaurant.

'You've suffered an injustice at Venstar. If that was—indirectly—my fault, I can only apologise. Unfortunately, the company's choice of candidate, however inappropriate, cannot be deprived of the job without good reason and establishing grounds takes time,' Andreo murmured dryly. 'In the short term it makes more sense for me to find a better position for you in another company.'

Pippa had grown very tense. 'I don't need your help—'

Andreo expelled his breath on an impatient hiss. 'I'm not offering help. I'm trying to redress a wrong. There's a subtle distinction.'

An uneasy flush had lit her cheekbones. She was convinced that he only felt he ought to intervene on her behalf because she had slept with him and that belief mortified her. 'What's done is done...I can look after myself—'

'I'd also like to see you achieve a status commensurate with your abilities—'

'Don't you think that I can manage that on my own?' Pippa was angry at being patronised. 'You're not responsible for me—'

'Maybe I *feel* responsible.' Andreo surveyed her with brooding dark eyes. 'But naturally I'll respect your wishes.'

Unexpectedly, amusement afflicted Pippa and melted her annoyance. 'Will you really? Even though you think my wishes are rubbish and you really hate people disagreeing with you? Will I have to grovel to get back in with you again?'

Andreo's appreciative gaze narrowed to a blazing sliver of raw gold. 'Just share my bed, *amore*. I've thought about nothing but you for thirty-six hours.'

Her mouth ran dry, a wanton flame lighting low in her pelvis.

'Are you hungry?' Andreo asked thickly.

'Not really but...' Her voice faded for Andreo had already sprung upright.

Three minutes later, he had swept her back out of the restaurant and settled her back into the limo. Without hesitation he had shown her that he would not allow conventional expectations to come between him and what he wanted. The atmosphere between them sizzled. She felt dizzy with wicked anticipation.

CHAPTER SIX

ANDREO had taken a penthouse apartment for the remainder of his stay in London.

He opened the door on the vast impressive hall, linked his lean fingers with Pippa's and walked her down to a bedroom as big as the entire ground floor of her home. She hovered in the centre of the carpet, suddenly desperately shy, realising that alcohol had blunted her inhibitions on the night of the party.

'Every time I look at you, I want to take your clothes off,' Andreo confided, shedding his tie and his jacket and tossing both aside with flattering enthusiasm.

She blushed to the roots of her hair. 'I'm glad I didn't know that at the meeting today. You seemed so distant.'

Andreo laughed huskily, strolling forward with easy assurance. 'Now you know why…I have a very active imagination. All guys are the same, *cara mia.*'

He untied her wrap top, took it off and tugged her closer. She kicked off her shoes, felt her skirt give at the waist as he unzipped it. When she stepped out of the skirt, he flipped her round, clamped her to his all-male muscular frame and crushed her mouth with passionate hunger below his.

That first sensual onslaught blew her away. His tongue delved between her lips in an elemental imitation of a much more sexual possession. Clinging to him, she shivered in the circle of his strong arms like a leaf in a high wind.

'I never knew I could feel like this...' Pippa whispered helplessly.

His lean, strong face was taut with intent. His shirt hung unbuttoned and loose to reveal a bronzed wedge of hair-roughened chest. He tasted her swollen mouth again while he reached behind her to undo her bra. When he lifted his proud dark head to look at her, her hands whipped up to cover herself but he caught them in his and drew them down again.

'I want to look at you,' he told her boldly.

Never had she been so conscious of being naked as she was standing there in front of Andreo, her bare breasts crested by shamelessly swollen pink nipples. 'Andreo...'

'*Dio mio*...you're even more exquisite than I remembered.' He sank down on the side of the bed and pulled her down onto his thighs.

At the first touch of his expert fingers on the tender crests straining for his attention, she gasped, weak and quivering with wanting. He closed a hand to the silken explosion of curls at the back of her head and tipped her over one arm. The heat of his mouth hungrily engulfed the throbbing pink buds to tug on the sensitive peaks. His hand cupped and shaped her pouting breasts, rubbing and teasing the stiff crests. The tormenting pleasure of his knowing exploration made her back arch. She moaned her response and speared shaking fingers into his cropped black hair.

He lifted her up and brought her down on the bed. Standing over her, he ran down the zip on his well-cut trousers. She lay there watching him, slim hips shifting in a restive motion against the spread below her. She was unbearably aware of the swollen moist heat at the heart of her. In one impatient movement, he dispensed with both trousers and boxers and the breath snarled up in her throat when she registered the extent of his fierce arousal.

'I want you *so* much, *cara*.' Like a lithe bronzed warrior ready for action, he came down on the bed beside her and skimmed a possessive hand over her tummy to trail along the edge of the modest white panties she wore. Leaning over her, he rearranged her so that he could remove that final garment. The hot gold of his eyes wandered at a leisurely pace over her rose-tipped breasts and the cluster of copper curls crowning her womanhood. There was a quiet sure confidence and sensual threat about his every move that made her burn and crave.

'You should wear jewel colours and silk. I shall buy you gorgeous lingerie, *amore*,' he murmured huskily.

'I wouldn't wear it...' she told him, shocked.

'You don't know all that I could make you do yet.' A slashing grin curved his beautiful mouth as he voiced that bold belief. 'Where did the wild adventuress at the party go?'

'Sorry?'

Golden eyes mocked her self-conscious colour. 'You stayed a good girl a long time...why me?'

The wicked amusement in his darkly attractive features was incredibly seductive. 'I like the way you kiss...'

Andreo drifted down closer, helplessly drawn by the warmth of her appreciation. 'Anything else, *amore*?'

A dreamy smile slid across her softened mouth. Just the whole incredible package, she thought helplessly and she wrapped her arms around him. 'I'm not telling...'

'Are you sure of that?' He shifted against her in a sinuous movement that sent her heart racing and her body quivering with wanton longing. She stretched up, the tender points of her breasts grazed by the rough black curls outlining his powerful pectoral muscles.

'You like *that*,' Andreo purred like a prowling, playful tiger, outlining her lower lip with the tip of his tongue and then penetrating between with a delicious force that stole everything she possessed.

'And that,' she confirmed shakily.

He ran his hand over her tummy to the nest of curls below and let his fingertips flirt there until she slid her thighs apart with a needy little moan. He stared down at her with smouldering sexy eyes of pure satisfaction. 'Do you know what I like best? That I'm the only guy you've ever had,' he confessed with primal force. 'You wouldn't believe how exciting I find that, *carissima*.'

'That's old-fashioned…' But even though she tried not to be, indeed reminded herself that theirs was only a casual affair, she was pleased by that confession. She was grateful that she hadn't ended up with a male who found her inexperience a bore.

'Maybe I'm an old-fashioned guy…deep down where it doesn't show,' Andreo affixed hastily, suddenly wondering where that strange thought had been born. Old-fashioned…him…since when? Since he had looked around his rarefied social circle and worked out that almost all the men had slept with the exact same women? Since he had decided that he did not want to marry a female who had trekked through all his friends' bedrooms as well?

'It doesn't show,' she whispered, shifting up to his caressing hand in helpless encouragement.

He skimmed the tiny sensitive spot below her feminine mound and dallied there with tormenting expertise. Suddenly she was no longer up to the challenge of speech. Breathing in irregular little fits and starts, her writhing body was on fire with a need that he alone controlled.

'Andreo…' she framed, awesomely aware of the rigid

hardness of his straining sex against her thigh, shivering with desire as the sweet, agonising ache of her craving became more than she could withstand in silence.

'It's OK...I can't wait either,' he breathed raggedly.

Rising over her, he sank his bold shaft into the slick wet heat of her and released a wondering groan of satisfaction. *'Amore...'*

Madly excited by him, she arched up to meet his powerful thrust. She couldn't get enough of him. Nothing had ever felt so good to her or so right. She tried to hold back the animalistic little cries wrenched from her as he drove her to his stormy sexual rhythm, but she couldn't. He sent her spiralling into a convulsive climax. Ecstasy sent her hurtling into wave on wave of exquisite sensation. His magnificent body shuddered and he vented a harsh groan of masculine satisfaction at the height of his own climax.

'You make me feel incredible, *amore*,' Andreo purred, stretching over her and then freeing her from his weight, only to haul her back to him with one strong arm. 'I want to have you again and again and again...I feel so greedy.'

Giddy, she hugged him tight until the world settled round her again and then she lay there sleepily smiling while he smoothed her tousled hair, told her how amazingly sexy those curls were and dropped tender kisses on any part of her within reach. She looked up at him with dazed eyes and there was a kind of fear in her then that she had not felt in years and years. What she had just experienced with him had been earth shattering passion and glorious fulfillment but sixth sense told her that she ought to ration herself on him.

'You're a very restful woman,' he teased, lifting her off the bed to accompany him into the opulent bathroom.

'Very mysterious too. Where, for instance, did you learn to speak colloquial French?'

'From my mother…she was born and bred in Paris.'

'Was the Frenchman who phoned you a relative?'

Pippa frowned in surprise. 'No, he's married to a friend. I've never quite taken to him—'

'But didn't I hear you arranging to meet him next week?'

'He asked me to visit his wife's favourite maternity shop with him and help him choose some outfits as a surprise for her.' Pippa sighed. 'I just couldn't credit that she was expecting yet another kid. That'll be number three and she's only twenty-three…'

Andreo had relaxed but he was ashamed of his own suspicions about her relationship with her friend's husband. He decided that he had met far too many calculating women, who would go to any lengths to capture a rich man whether they wanted him or not.

Pippa watched him switch on the power shower in the big cubicle and simply reach for her again. He acted as if he owned her but what shook her most was that she liked him acting that way. He was protective and, when he wanted to be, gentle in a way she had never associated with his sex, especially with a guy who was so innately masculine and aggressive at other times. He made her feel like a cross between a spun glass ornament in need of constant care and a sexual enchantress because he couldn't even share the shower with her without getting aroused again.

He was her perfect dream guy. She had not been wrong about that. He was gorgeous, fantastic in bed and he treated her as though she was as irresistible as Cleopatra. It was no wonder she was already halfway to being infatuated. Given very little encouragement, she thought in shrinking dismay, she would fall head over heels in love with him and make a complete ass of herself!

'We'll order in some food...I don't think I could be trusted in a public place with you yet, *bella mia*.' Having enfolded her in a fleecy towel, he lifted her hands and pressed his lips to the centre of each palm, looking down at her from beneath dense black lashes longer than her own with a provocative gleam in his teasing gaze. 'But I've got you all evening and all night...'

Pippa tensed, imagining sleeping in his arms, waking up with him and deciding that she could not indulge herself in that amount of intimacy with him. 'I'm not staying the night,' she told him in a rush.

'Why not?' One arm carelessly curved round her, Andreo was already punching out a number on the phone by the bed.

'I don't stay the night...I mean, I...prefer to go home to my own bed,' she declared.

Andreo slung the phone back down. 'How would you know what you prefer? I've got to be the first guy you've stayed with—'

'I just prefer it...OK?' She worried at her lower lip anxiously.

His strong bone structure taut, Andreo veiled his fulminating gaze and wondered if his own sins were coming home to roost. As a rule, he never invited his lovers to stay the night. Staying over added a whole different dimension to a relationship and he liked to keep things casual. So why had he invited her?

'No problem.' Jaw-line at an aggressive angle, Andreo ordered in Thai food without asking her what she wanted.

Luckily, Pippa adored Thai food. Sitting cross-legged on a big swanky sofa, clad in a towelling robe, she ate

with appetite and she asked Andreo how he had come to
have a brother so much younger than he was.

'Marco was a surprise package when my mother was
in her forties. My father died when he was five, so Marco
turns to me a lot,' Andreo said. 'We have three older
sisters, all married, all very given to spoiling little broth-
ers and he was turning into a horrible precocious brat.
So I persuaded Mama to send him away to school. He's
much improved.'

'What was it like being one of five children?' she
prompted curiously.

'Fun…it would've been more fun, though, if a couple
of the bossy sisters had been boys,' he drawled with
mockery. 'Some day I'd like a big family.'

Pippa gave him a startled look. 'I don't want kids at
all,' she confided without thinking, reacting to her own
surprise that a guy like Andreo D'Alessio could admit to
such an unfashionable ambition.

Andreo was frowning. 'You don't want kids…*any*?'

Feeling awkward, she added with rather forced amusement, 'I'm more into my career.'

'So what are you planning to do if I have got you
pregnant?' Andreo enquired with a derisive edge to his
dark, deep drawl.

Pippa paled. 'That's not going to happen…why are
you saying that?'

'Because after that mishap on the contraceptive front
the night before last, it's a distinct possibility and I'd
appreciate knowing right now up front,' Andreo incised
with angry emphasis, 'what the score is likely to be if
you *do* conceive!'

Pippa pushed away her plate and scrambled off the
sofa. Her restive fingers worked feverishly at the robe's

over-long sleeves, which were threatening to engulf her hands. 'I don't like this conversation.'

'*Per meraviglia!* You think I do? But I've asked a fair question,' Andreo bit out rawly.

Furious with him, mortified and feeling threatened by the subject under discussion, Pippa spun on her heel and headed back to the bedroom. Gathering up her clothes in haste, she hurried into the bathroom.

Before she could get the door shut, however, Andreo appeared, lean, powerful face set hard. 'I think that you could give me an answer...'

'How can I answer a crazy question like that?' Pippa almost sobbed at him in her discomfiture and distress. She had made what was for her a casual admission and had without the smallest warning found herself plunged deep into moral issues that she had never had to consider before. His contemptuous attitude both hurt and infuriated her.

Locking the door behind her, she pulled on her clothes, tears lashing her eyes.

When she emerged, Andreo had also got dressed. Drop dead gorgeous in a silver-grey shirt and black cargo trousers, he strode forward, a look of cool exasperation in his scrutiny. 'This is insane, *cara*—'

'Well, don't look at *me* when you say that! I want to go home...I've called a taxi.' Sidestepping him, Pippa fled out into the hall.

'I'm not letting you go like this. Perhaps I shouldn't have said anything...but how was I to know it was such a controversial subject?' Andreo threw up lean brown hands to accentuate his astonishment. 'Most women *like* babies!'

Pippa wanted to slap him. 'I like babies too...I just don't want one of my own!'

Andreo strode across the wide glossy hall floor and rested his hands on her rigid shoulders. She was trembling. 'You'll change your mind—'

'No, I won't!' she told him fiercely.

She pulled away from him. Her mind had already thrown her way back to memories she rarely visited and lodged on a painful image of her mother crying and calling herself a rotten mother because she had been unable to make theirs a happy home.

Andreo settled scorching golden eyes on Pippa's pale, frozen profile. The intercom by the front door buzzed.

'That'll be my taxi...'

'Walk out now and I won't phone you tomorrow,' Andreo threatened without hesitation. 'If you walk, we're finished.'

To her everlasting shame, Pippa stopped dead in her tracks.

Andreo spoke into the intercom and said that she would be down in a few minutes.

Coming to a halt behind her, he closed both arms round her. She went stiff, resisting him with every fibre of her will-power, but the weakening started like a melting sensation deep down inside her. She wanted this guy. She wanted to be with him and she wanted his good opinion too, which was why it hurt to lose it over an issue that struck her as being as crazily remote as the risk of pregnancy. 'I've already told you...it's not that easy to fall pregnant...are you listening to me?' she demanded sharply.

'*Sì*. I'm listening.'

'My mother was never able to conceive again after she had me and my grandmother tried for ten years before she had my mother!' she protested feverishly.

'That doesn't mean that you're likely to have similar problems.'

As the fierce tension holding her rigid began to give she curved back into his lean, powerful frame. She was of too practical a nature to sustain an argument about a situation that she could not imagine developing. Andreo slowly turned her round to face him. He splayed long fingers to her taut cheekbones. 'You scare me...you scare yourself, *amore*—'

She didn't know why but the wretched tears just broke free then and cascaded down her cheeks. With a driven groan, he hauled her close and she choked back a sob, drinking in the gloriously familiar scent of him like an addict. 'You're too serious,' she told him chokily. 'Just looking for trouble is like asking for it.'

Molten gold eyes assailed hers. 'Come back to bed...'

'My taxi...'

He pressed her down on the fancy wrought-iron chaise longue ornamenting the hall and called the doorman in the foyer. She sat there shivering, shocked at the woman she was somehow changing into against her own volition. She had said she was going home. She should have carried through on what she had said she would do. Andreo swung back to her, all male, powered by resolute determination that mocked her own. While he'd been on the phone, he had unbuttoned his shirt again. He stood there in front of her and simply shed his clothes where he stood.

'I want to go home for the night,' she mumbled unsteadily, sounding like a little child trying to talk herself into running away.

Slowly he raised her to her feet. She hovered, letting him peel off her garments one by one.

'No, you don't...you want to be with me, *amore*.

Walking away was tearing you up,' Andreo reminded her with lethal assurance, and then he bent and caught her up into his arms to power back towards the bedroom. 'Week nights, you can go home, but weekends you're mine from start to finish. Sorry, but that's how it is.'

'It's a Thursday,' she muttered weakly into the smooth brown shoulder she was already pressing her lips against.

'Sorry, I didn't hear that...'

'It's Thursday.'

In the act of arranging her on the bed with the care of a connoisseur, Andreo elevated an incredulous black brow at that announcement. 'You need to consult a calendar, *cara mia.*'

'It *feels* like a Friday night,' she whispered in sudden decision, surrendering to his sheer animal vibrancy and ferocious resolve and amply rewarded by his lazy smile of approbation.

Pippa plucked a coral-pink rose from Andreo's latest floral offering and wedged it into the buttonhole on her new blue jacket. Matched with a slim short skirt and fitted to her small waist, it gave her figure a flattering definition that she was unused to seeing.

Her terraced home was awash with flowers that perfumed every room. At least once every couple of nights she had made a supreme effort to tear herself from Andreo's side around dawn and visit home to obtain fresh clothes. She would always bring back all the flowers he gave her and arrange them into vases. In the hall mirror she studied her reflection, absorbing the happiness in her eyes and the silly smile that just the thought of Andreo summoned up. Tension compressed her lips then instead. Indeed she gave herself a stern look. In little more than thirty six hours she would be flying off to France, not only to enjoy her holiday with Tabby and Christien, but also to take her first step towards forging a fresh existence. But leaving Andreo promised to be the toughest thing she had ever had to do...

Yet wouldn't that only be because most ironically *she* would be the one to get in first and end their affair? Andreo had not yet betrayed any sign of boredom with her and why should he have? On her terms, the past nine days had been full of fun and passion and special moments. She was determined not to forget a single second that she had spent with him and had committed every single detail with religious care into her diary. However, nine days were also a very short period of time and she reckoned that Andreo had decided that it would be more convenient for him if he simply let their affair continue until the date of his own return to Italy arrived. Of course, as she had not even told him yet about her own plans, he still had no idea that she was on the very brink of leaving both Venstar and London herself.

Why hadn't she told him? Perhaps she had been afraid that if he knew he might seek to replace her with someone who would be available for a little longer. At least she wasn't fool enough to start imagining that someone as essentially ordinary as she was could possibly have any hope of a more lasting future with a male of Andreo's legendary reputation.

No, she had made the sensible decision that she would make the utmost of every precious minute of her time with him but neither look for nor indeed hope for anything more. In return for her common-sense outlook, her careful, honest acceptance of her own limitations, she had had nine incredibly wonderful days living a fantasy existence with a guy whom...a guy of whom she had become very, *very* fond. That was all. Only a very stupid

woman would have let herself fall in love with Andreo
D'Alessio. And she wasn't stupid, was she?

A limo was waiting at the kerb when she emerged from
her home. Quite unconscious of the curtains twitching at
the neighbours' houses, she scrambled in and called
Andreo on the car phone.

'I told you I'd get the train,' she scolded softly.

'I want you to conserve your energy for me...I'll see
you at one for lunch.'

Even his rich, dark, accented drawl sent a little responsive quiver down her spine. 'Hmm...' She smiled
while she thought about how much she enjoyed eating
out in the exotic restaurants at discreet locations that
Andreo chose for their daily assignations. 'Can't wait.'

A sudden silence seemed to fall when she reached her
desk at Venstar. But then of recent she had progressed
from being the first to start work in the morning to being
the last to arrive and the first to leave. Furthermore, since
the simple work she was currently being allotted was way
below her capabilities she was free to daydream as much
as she liked.

'You know that's a really fantastic suit you're wearing...it's *so* funky!' Jonelle commented rather loudly.

Pippa gave the blonde a sunny smile of abstraction. 'I
think so too.'

Her colleague cleared her throat. 'It looks very like a
Versace outfit I saw in a shop window last week. Is it...I
mean, Versace?'

Pippa shrugged without interest for she had never been
into fashion. 'I don't know. I haven't looked at the label,'
she said truthfully.

After all, Andreo had presented the outfit to her with
the far more interesting news that he had *had* to buy it
because it was the exact shade of her eyes. Apparently

he had stopped the limo in traffic and got out the instant he'd seen it, so very probably the suit had featured in a window display. Whatever, Pippa kept on seeing a dazzling image of Andreo casting aside all cool sophistication and shouting at his chauffeur to stop and she thought such impetuous behaviour was incredibly romantic. It would have been true to say that had Andreo bought her a garment adorned with zebra stripes she would have been so affected by his going to so much trouble on her behalf that she would have worn it out of gratitude.

At that abstracted response, Jonelle and her equally inquisitive fellow listeners stared at Pippa in near disbelief.

'You're also wearing Jimmy Choo shoes,' Jonelle dared, gazing enviously at the strappy works of art adorning Pippa's slender feet.

'The heel snapped off my shoe when I was out for lunch yesterday,' Pippa confided.

'I wonder if my heel snapped off would a total miracle take place in the street for little old me!' With that acid comment, Cheryl shot Pippa a look of sullen resentment before she stalked out of the office.

Cheryl's spiteful attempts to upset and humiliate Pippa and provoke her into leaving Venstar had got her nowhere, for in the mood that Pippa had been in of late, she would not have noticed Cheryl had she stood on her head and screamed. In vain did Cheryl complain about the very long lunch hours that Pippa now took. Pippa would mutter something vague about having lost track of the time and drift off looking very much as though she was existing on another mental plane entirely.

Minutes later, Andreo's brother, Marco, phoned Pippa. It had to be about the sixth time he had called her. On the first few occasions he had asked for help with maths assignments, but since then their dealings had become more casually friendly and his latest request was for advice on what to buy for a six-year-old niece's birthday. Ten minutes later, Jonelle answered the phone ringing on Cheryl's desk and went off in search of the brunette. When neither Cheryl nor Ricky were to be found, Pippa received a call from a director asking her to go to the meeting room on the top floor to make herself available in Cheryl's place for the client due to arrive.

In the act of stepping into the lift she discovered that Andreo was stepping out. Although it was only a matter of hours since they had last seen each other, she still could not drag her attention from his hard, handsome bone structure and she was utterly ensnared when she met his riveting dark golden eyes.

'Is it long until lunch time?' Pippa muttered, having left her watch behind in his bedroom.

Andreo lifted a lean hand and brushed a stray curl back from her cheekbone with a slow, heart-stopping smile. 'Too long…where are you heading?'

'The meeting room. Lester Saunders is due to arrive and Miss Long can't be contacted.'

'That could be Venstar's biggest advantage over the competition,' Andreo drawled with cutting dark humour, following her back into the lift to accompany her.

Minutes later, Andreo pushed back the door to allow Pippa to precede him into the comfortable room set aside for important appointments.

Halfway into the room, she stopped dead to gape at the man and woman writhing in passion on the sofa. Ricky Brownlow pulled himself up in consternation when he saw Pippa but his partner, Cheryl, gave Pippa a defiant look. 'Don't you know when to make yourself scarce?'

'Don't you?' Andreo breathed smooth as silk when he

strolled forward into view and proceeded to sack the guilty couple for gross misconduct.

Pippa had not even suspected that Ricky, who was a married man, and Cheryl might have been having an affair. While they slunk out, Pippa straightened the room for the client's imminent arrival.

'You were shocked. You really don't listen to the rumour mill, do you?' Andreo murmured. 'Even I had heard that Brownlow was believed to have pushed Cheryl for your job because it would make it easier for them to spend time together. It only remains for me to appoint you back to Acting Finance Manager—'

Pippa stiffened. 'No...no, I don't want it now. Not this way and not when you and I are...er...involved.'

Andreo quirked a questioning brow. 'That's not a sensible decision.'

'I think that's *my*—'

'No, you should start thinking like the career woman that you keep on telling me you are, *cara*,' Andreo countered with sardonic bite, and left her.

While Pippa dealt with Lester Saunders, however, she asked herself why it was that she had automatically rejected the job that she had longed to have just two short weeks earlier. Was she that committed to her plans to relocate in France? Or had Cheryl's appointment soured her on the idea of remaining at Venstar? Whatever, she could see that she did owe Andreo an explanation. After all, hadn't she told him that he was responsible for her loss of promotion? Naturally he wanted her to accept the position that he believed should have been hers in the first instance.

As soon as she was free, Pippa headed off to see Andreo, only to be told that he was busy and that she would have to wait. She took a seat and wished she had simply phoned Andreo direct instead of going through businesslike motions.

The receptionist leant across her desk to whisper confidentially, 'I shouldn't say but Mr D'Alessio is with his girlfriend. Apparently she's just back from working abroad.'

'Really?' Jolted and then realising that she could only be hearing office gossip, Pippa grinned. 'Tell me more.'

'She's Lili Richards...you know the famous model. You wouldn't *believe* how breathtaking she looks in the flesh!'

'Lili Richards...' Pippa had never heard of her.

'You could see how close she and Mr D'Alessio are.'

Pippa's interested smile had grown a little fixed round the edges. 'Could you?'

'Yes. The minute she saw him, she just dived on him. A reaction most of us could sympathise with. Let's face it, he's to die for,' the receptionist said dreamily. 'And with his wild reputation, I bet she's been worried sick that he would find someone else while she was away...'

Pippa's mobile pulsed in her pocket. She took it out. It was Andreo calling and her tension dissolved. Honestly, an attractive woman visited him and the office grapevine went mental on colourful rumours!

'I can't make lunch,' Andreo informed her without any preamble.

Pippa's brow indented. 'But I wanted to talk to you—'

'Unfortunately, some business has come up. I'll call you later...OK?'

Pippa opened her dry mouth but no sound emerged.

'OK?' Andreo prompted, sounding cool, distant and impatient.

'OK,' she almost croaked and he rang off.

Her hand trembling, Pippa put her mobile back in her pocket and slowly rose upright.

'The boss and Lili Richards are about to leave!' the receptionist was gasping into the phone for someone else's benefit.

No, she wasn't going to hang about behaving like a possessive girlfriend who didn't trust him. She began to move down the corridor. All along it heads were emerging from offices. Every employee on the floor seemed to be angling to get a first-hand look at Andreo and his visitor. Pippa backed into a clump of indoor plants and hovered. He had said he had business and if he said he had business, she believed him because she trusted him absolutely. She was only hanging around to celebrity-spot.

Andreo strode into view and hit the lift button. He was not alone. A woman who looked even to Pippa's unappreciative gaze like a fantasy pin-up was clinging to his arm. She had a mane of baby blonde hair and flawless features. She was just beautiful, just really, really, really beautiful, Pippa conceded in a daze. A famous model, yes, she looked as if she would be famous. There was something unearthly about someone that beautiful who did not even seem to be wearing make-up. Something rather sick-making too…

Maybe Lili Richards was really spoilt and had made it difficult for Andreo to avoid taking her out to lunch. Maybe she was a client, a family friend…a sister, cousin, childhood playmate? Maybe Andreo had been bullied into it. Maybe he was being kidnapped.

While Pippa watched, Lili slid caressing hands beneath Andreo's suit jacket with the familiarity of a lover confident of her welcome. Making it patently obvious that she couldn't keep her sex-starved hands off him, she stretched up to kiss him with similar enthusiasm…at which point Pippa could no longer stand to look.

'Looks like they're headed for the nearest bed!' she heard someone laugh.

Forty seconds later, Pippa was horribly sick in the cloakroom. She reeled dizzily back from the cubicle wall and struggled to get a grip on herself. But indelibly etched on her mind's eye was Andreo and his girlfriend. Two very beautiful human beings perfectly matched. Dear heaven, how could she have believed in him, trusted him? Pippa Plain…just when had she allowed herself to forget that that was her nickname?

Feeling like a robot, she freshened up as best she could and went off to clear her desk.

'Is it true that Ricky and Cheryl have been sacked?' Jonelle gushed.

'Yes.'

'So you'll be the new manager, then,' Jonelle assumed.

'I don't want the job any more.'

'Of course…you're seeing Mr D'Alessio,' the blonde murmured soft and low and admiring.

Pippa froze.

'We worked out it was you at the party by the second bunch of flowers,' Jonelle confided with an appreciative giggle. 'You really know how to surprise people, don't you?'

'Yeah…I just dumped him,' Pippa responded, wondering how long it would take for word of Lili's existence to work back to the finance section.

She went home and phoned HR to tell them that no, sorry, do what they will, she wasn't coming back *ever*. Then she undressed and put the designer suit, the shoes and all the dripping flowers and the cards she had saved into a bin bag. Pulling out a couple of suitcases, she

began to pack. Unable to tolerate even the minor risk of
Andreo trying to see her again, she decided to check into
a hotel for the night. But before she left her home, she
had the bin-bag collected for delivery to Andreo's apartment. Not that she imagined that either he or Lili would
get out of bed to answer the doorbell.

CHAPTER SEVEN

PIPPA leant on the ancient stone balustrade bounding the shaded terrace at Duvernay and tried to suppress all her unhappy and self-pitying thoughts in appreciation of the wonderful views stretching in every direction.

The château's glorious formal gardens were surrounded by rolling green fields that in turn gave way to apple orchards said to produce some of the best cider in the world. The remainder of the vast Duvernay estate, the ancestral home of Tabby's husband, Christien Laroche, was the equivalent of a densely wooded nature reserve. But only a few miles to the west lay the jagged Breton coastline of rocky cliffs, sandy coves and picturesque fishing ports.

Her fabulous bedroom suite was worthy of a five star hotel and she had been royally entertained. For two long weeks she had done her best to put on a cheerful front for her hosts' benefit, for who wanted to entertain a miserable, weepy guest? Unfortunately, being in the company of a very happy married couple had only made her feel more betrayed, more alone and more depressed.

Christien Laroche had been incredibly nice to her. In fact Tabby's husband had been so much kinder than the rather arrogant character whom Pippa had recalled from the past that she had honestly wondered whether Christien had guessed that his wife's childhood friend was suffering from a broken heart.

Yes, Pippa was no longer kidding herself: she had fallen madly in love with Andreo. She had pretended she

was in control when she was not. But common sense told
her why she had never actually got around to making
arrangements to let her London home and why she had
been waiting to the last possible minute to hand in her
notice at Venstar. It would only have taken one encour-
aging word from Andreo to persuade her to drop any idea
of making a permanent move to France. Neither her pride
nor her intelligence had got a look-in when it came to
Andreo D'Alessio.

While his lovely girlfriend had been abroad and un-
available, Andreo had used Pippa to fill the vacancy in
his bed and satisfy his sexual needs. She despised herself
for having surrendered her body so easily. What had
seemed so very special now seemed cheap and tawdry.
Andreo had lied about being free of other entanglements
but then as she was well aware many otherwise upright
men thought nothing of the lies that went hand in hand
with infidelity. And she could not accuse Andreo of having promised her love or any kind of a future.

So why on earth had Andreo repeatedly attempted to
contact her since she had left London? Surely he had
guessed that she had found out about Lili? Yet he had
initially texted her innumerable times. When that had
failed to draw a response he had left half a dozen messages on her mobile phone. Messages that had sounded
genuinely anxious about her apparent vanishing act.
What on earth had he been playing at? Had the dustbin
bag she sent him not been explanation enough? She had
changed her phone number but had reluctantly passed on
her new one to Marco when he had begged as hard as a
fourteen-year-old boy could beg not to be made to pay
for his big brother's sins.

Tabby wandered out onto the terrace with a pretty tod-
dler maternally anchored to one hip. While her five-year-

old son, Jake, bore a close resemblance to his darkly
handsome father, Jolie, her one-year-old daughter, had
her mother's toffee-coloured hair and lively green eyes.

'I *love* this dress.' Tabby smoothed an appreciative
hand over the garment chosen by her friend from her
favourite maternity shop, for it was styled to flatter the
rounded shape of a woman more than four months pregnant. 'I'm so grateful you went shopping with Christien.
Left to himself, he always goes for fancy formal stuff
and in this climate I prefer casual and comfortable.'

'The summers here are warm.' Pippa tossed her damp
hair with her hand to cool the nape of her neck. In the
act of tilting her head back, she was assailed by a sudden
giddiness that forced her to steady herself on the balustrade with both hands.

Oh, dear, she thought fearfully, lashes lowering to conceal the anxious look clouding her eyes. More than a
week had already passed since she had first noted that
her period was late in arriving, an event unusual enough
to rouse her concern. In addition, she had felt rather
queasy on several occasions. Now she had had a minor
dizzy spell. She knew the most common signs of pregnancy as well as most young women. However, she also
suspected that her emotional highs and lows and even
worry might well be making her imagine symptoms and
could also have interfered with her system.

'You like Christien better than you used to, don't you?'
Tabby prompted with amused satisfaction.

Dredging herself from her uneasy thoughts, Pippa
smiled. 'I've only really got the chance to get to know
him properly since I came to stay.'

'He's so confident that he used to set your teeth on
edge and I can understand that after the way your dad
treated your mum and you.' Tabby sighed with sympa-

thy. 'I don't blame you for distrusting men with strong characters.'

Pippa was disconcerted because Tabby seemed to be alluding to an issue that Pippa had believed was a Stevenson family secret.

Reading her friend's expression, Tabby winced. 'Oh, no, you didn't realise I knew about—'

'Dad and his other women?' Pippa strove to look unconcerned.

Tabby grimaced. 'My stepmother let the cat out of the bag during that awful final holiday. Her flirting with your father to annoy mine didn't exactly add to the friendly atmosphere. I felt so sorry for your mother.'

'She was a gentle soul and miserable with Dad.' Pippa discovered that she could feel almost grateful for the opportunity to finally express her pain on her late mother's behalf. She would never forget overhearing her father telling her mother that he was entitled to stray when he had such an unattractive wife. 'He could say very cruel things.'

'It was his way of controlling you and your mum,' Tabby opined. 'But a man can be strong without needing to hurt and humiliate women.'

'I know that.' But Pippa was only agreeing in the hope that that would conclude a subject that went too close to the bone for comfort. There had been nothing weak about Andreo, but that had not prevented him from hurting and humiliating her, she reflected painfully.

'Do you?' Tabby gave her a troubled look. 'Or has your dad's big, scary shadow fallen over your relationship with the Italian bloke you won't tell me about?'

'I just had a fight with…Andreo…no big deal,' Pippa quipped with forced lightness of tone, because her fierce pride would not allow her to confess the truth to Tabby,

who was secure in her husband's obvious love for her
and their children.

Starved of even such minor facts by her friend's re-
served nature, Tabby could not hide the strength of her
desire to know more. 'Did you even give Andreo the
chance to say sorry?'

Pippa went pink with discomfiture and then decided to
tell a little white lie for the sake of peace. 'Actually...we're talking again. He phoned me last night—'

'Oh, that's marvellous!' Tabby gave her much taller
friend a delighted hug of approbation. 'I wish Christien
and I could get the chance to meet him...'

At that opportune moment, Jolie tugged at Pippa's cotton trousers and provided a welcome distraction by holding up her arms to be lifted. Pippa looked down into the
little girl's trusting gaze and sunny smile and obliged.
Jolie had all the confidence of a child who was growing
up in an atmosphere of love and contentment. Pippa reckoned that granted the same background to her childhood
she herself would have developed a healthier self-esteem.

'Come and play cars,' Jake urged in turn. 'Jolie can
watch.'

Tabby rested most afternoons but it was her nanny's
day off and she looked tired. Ignoring her half-hearted
protests, Pippa took the children back indoors to give her
friend a break.

After dinner that evening, Pippa thanked Christien and
Tabby for their wonderful hospitality. In the morning she
planned to board a train to the Dordogne to visit her
mother's burial place for the first time. Following that
she would head to Paris and seek accommodation and a
new job. Christien had already offered her the use of his
Paris apartment and lucrative employment, but Pippa pre-

ferred not to mix friendship with the acceptance of favours she could not return.

'Do you think I could persuade Hilary to come for a visit?' Tabby asked wistfully outside Pippa's bedroom door.

'She'd love to come, but between her little sister and the hair salon, she's very tied down,' Pippa explained ruefully. 'I wish one of us had heard from Jen but she seems to have disappeared off the face of the earth.'

'She was always very shy but I'm sure she'll get in touch eventually. In the meantime, you and me and Hilary should plan a proper get-together for the new year,' Tabby suggested before she said goodnight to Pippa.

Pippa was emerging from the shower when she heard a helicopter coming in to land. There was nothing unusual in that. The owner of an international airline, Christien flew himself most places and so did many of his social circle.

Clad in a cool white cotton nightdress, Pippa was setting out clothes for the morning when a hasty knock sounded on the door and Tabby appeared wreathed in a big grin. 'I've got a fantastic surprise for you!' her friend carolled like an excited schoolgirl. 'Close your eyes!'

Suppressing a sigh, Pippa did as she was asked. 'Can I open them yet?'

'Not until you hear the door close again...and don't feel you have to hurry down for breakfast in the morning!' Tabby giggled.

As the door snapped shut Pippa was picturing a beaker of hot chocolate topped with melted marshmallows or some such sentimental reminder of their childhood. But when her lashes swept up she got a severe shock. Instead of a soothing night drink, Tabby had delivered a six-foot-five-inch male to her guest's bedroom.

'Tabby's very sweet,' Andreo murmured smooth as black ice.

Just one look at him and Pippa felt as if she had been knifed. He was the male she had craved against her will for two endless weeks. The male she had simultaneously craved and hated, whom she had last seen being pawed by the beautiful Lili. Her tummy flipped in rejection of the cruel images flooding her memory. Angry pain was no true barrier against his hard male beauty and that raw physicality of his that made her senses sing. His charcoal grey business suit was tailored to a designer fit over his broad shoulders, lean hips and long, powerful thighs. He looked totally spectacular and her mouth ran dry.

'How the heck did you find out where I was?' she demanded fiercely. 'I didn't tell anyone!'

'When you were last on the phone to Marco, he heard someone address you in French—'

'I'll never forgive him for telling you—'

'Be fair, *bella mia*. You only asked him not to divulge your new phone number and he did respect that. I had to lean on him a little before he mentioned hearing French being spoken—'

Pippa dealt him an aghast look of reproach. 'You bully...he's only fourteen!'

'And even at that tender age, Marco has a healthy regard for family honour and loyalty,' Andreo delivered dryly.

'You still haven't explained how you discovered I was here—'

'I had your background investigated—'

Pippa stared back at him in disbelief. 'You did... *what?*'

'You have strong connections to France through your own family tree. Your friendship with Tabby and Christien Laroche made this an obvious port of call—'

'I can't believe that you dared to come here—'

'I dare…believe it, *amore*,' Andreo incised.

'Nor can I imagine what crazy stories you told to talk your way through the door—'

Andreo dealt her a look of hauteur. 'What need had I to tell stories? Your friend seemed unsurprised to see me,' he stated grimly. '*Santo Cielo*…I had only to say who I was and she offered to take me up to your room!'

Severe embarrassment claimed Pippa. Her own little white lie about Andreo having phoned the night before to heal their differences had come back to haunt her. Naturally Tabby had assumed that Andreo's arrival would be a wonderful surprise for Pippa and that she herself was helping along a lovers' reconciliation.

Brilliant golden eyes clung to her fast-reddening face. 'Care to explain that? Or am I supposed to assume that every guy who calls here asking for you is shown straight up to your bedroom, no questions asked?'

Infuriated by that dig, which pierced right to the heart of her belief that she had already made an enormous fool of herself over him, Pippa lost her temper and swung up her hand.

'*Don't…*' Closing lean fingers round her wrist before she could deliver that potential slap, Andreo sent her a hard look of censure and voiced that single word with icy restraint.

Pippa retrieved her arm from his hold, rage and mortification united inside her now. She was so mad with him that she could hardly catch her breath to speak. 'Get out of here, then!'

'No…' His refusal was cool and level.

'Then I'll move to another room...'

'If you like...I'll fish my bedtime reading out of my case and settle down for the night,' Andreo murmured soft and smooth.

Temper had taken Pippa to the door, but at those words that seemed to offer an unknown threat she stilled, her brow indenting. 'What are you talking about?'

Reaching past her, Andreo opened the door, swept up the leather case and garment bags draped over it and lifted them into the room.

'Andreo?' Pippa queried in bewilderment, unable to comprehend why he should suddenly remove the pressure on her and behave as if what she did was immaterial to him.

'You don't appear to grasp how angry I am with you,' he breathed in sudden warning. 'You owe me an explanation and a grovelling apology—'

Pippa folded her arms with a jerk. 'I don't think so.'

'And in the absence of said grovelling apology, I am likely to sink as low as a guy can sink—'

'Tell me something I don't know! I've already seen you swarming all over your blonde girlfriend!' Pippa suddenly slung at him with such feeling rage and pain that her voice had a crack in it.

Andreo studied her with fixed attention, eyes a shimmering gold below spiky black lashes. 'Correction. She was swarming over me. So you *did* see me with Lili. I wondered about that—'

'You said you couldn't go out for lunch with me because you had business to take care of...some business!' Pippa bawled at him full throttle.

'Lili was with me when I phoned you. Within her hearing I could hardly tell you that I was taking her out to lunch to dump her.'

To dump her? *To dump her?* Those magical words echoed in ringing decibels through Pippa's brain and made it quite impossible for her to think of anything else. He had been planning to *end* his relationship with Lili Richards?

Andreo sent her a grim glance. 'Of course, had you stayed in the same building, not to mention the same country you would have found that fact out for yourself because I would have brought you up to speed on events when I saw you that night.'

Momentarily, Pippa had been silenced. She had to angle back against the high bed for support because her legs felt shaky. Andreo had chosen her in preference to that gorgeous blonde fantasy woman? As a statement of intent, it was almost more than she could credit and then a little native wit crept back in to remind her that he had sworn that he was free of involvement with any other woman.

'You lied to me,' Pippa condemned. 'When we first met I asked if you were involved with anyone else and you said no.'

'As far as I was concerned it was true. Lili knew she would be travelling for a couple of months. Our relationship was casual. We agreed that if either of us met anyone else we would be free to follow it up. I met you. Lili said she met no one, but I suspect that what she really meant was that she met no one worth mentioning,' Andreo completed with rich cynicism.

So, according to his version of events, Lili had just existed in the background of his life, a casual bed partner when she'd been physically available. Surely that was all that she, Pippa, could have been to him as well? Had she not originally decided to allow their relationship to run only until she left for France? Hadn't that been the most sensible attitude? After all, Andreo was not looking for a long-term relationship with her either. It was better to be the one leaving than the one who was left.

In any case, how could she trust a word he said about Lili Richards? Since when was it possible to believe anything a man said when it came to the *other* woman in his life? How many times had her late father lied to her trusting mother and persuaded her that an affair had been over when it had been in fact still continuing? Or even that his extra-marital activities had existed in her mother's imagination alone? How many times had he voiced arguments that had sounded credible but that had eventually turned out to be cruel, unfeeling lies?

'Any comment?' Andreo murmured flatly.

Pippa shot him a driven glance, imagining how she would feel watching him leave her again only to recoil from that prospect. No matter how bitter and suspicious she was, she still had to fight a demeaning desire to keep him with her. Ashamed of her weakness, she tilted her chin. 'Coming here was a waste of your time!'

Andreo frowned. 'I don't believe I've ever had a more one-sided dialogue with a woman. You don't even appreciate what you've done.'

'What *I've* done?' Pippa echoed with incredulity.

'*Sì*. Without a word of warning or explanation to anyone, you vanished into thin air—'

'I handed in my notice and I returned your gifts…didn't that all speak for itself?'

'That you were annoyed about something? Didn't it once cross your mind that when you disappeared I'd be worried sick about you?'

Pippa jerked up a rebellious shoulder. 'Why should it have done?'

Savage anger flared in Andreo's censorious gaze and

he moved closer. 'We were in a relationship. I gave you no reason to believe that I would do anything to hurt or betray you. *Dio mio*...you trusted me enough to give me a key to your home!'

Her throat closing over on a flood of tears, Pippa focused on a point to one side of him for she did not want to be reminded of how easily she had initially given her trust.

'When you didn't answer my messages I went to your home to check that you weren't lying there ill. I could see that you had packed and left in a hurry and that remained a source of genuine anxiety to me.'

Involuntarily, Pippa glanced up and encountered scorching golden eyes of contempt that froze her to the spot.

'At that point I had no idea that you had already terminated your employment with Venstar. Concern prompted me to hire private investigators in an effort to trace your movements. Of course, a less honourable guy would just have sat down and opened your diary and read it from start to finish!'

Those final terrifying words hung there in the air while Pippa stared back at Andreo as if he had just developed horns and cloven feet. Every scrap of colour had ebbed from her face. 'My...my diary? You *know* I keep a diary?'

'It was hard to miss. There it was beside your bed—bright pink and furry and adorned with the words, ''My diary'' and a tiny girlie padlock which I could break with one finger.' Andreo seemed to positively savour that description and assurance.

'You saw my diary...' Pippa was sick with horror at him having got that close to her every written secret thought, especially when her every written secret thought had recently related to him. Why had she given him the key to her home? Why had she not had the wit to hide her diary away?

'Saw it and lifted it—'

'Lifted it?' Pippa gasped strickenly.

'It's just amazing the way you're finally giving me the attention I deserve, *cara mia*,' Andreo remarked silkily.

Pippa was paralysed to the spot. 'Did you break the padlock?'

'Not as yet but it strikes me as the most straightforward solution to your refusal to talk—'

'I'm not refusing to talk...where's my diary?' she steeled herself to demand.

'In my case—'

'You brought it with you?'

Andreo gave her a silent nod of confirmation.

Pippa breathed in very deep and thought fast but there was just no way out that she could see. 'I'll do just about anything to stop you reading my diary.'

'That's what I reckoned too,' Andreo confided, deadpan.

'Will you just give it back to me?' she prompted very softly and gently.

'No. Right now, it's a negotiating tool and a guarantee that you think and listen and eventually account for your behaviour,' Andreo delineated without hesitation.

Her teeth gritted and her fingernails flexed and bit into her palms.

'But in the short term, I'm willing to grant you a little breathing space. After all, it's late, we're in someone else's home and you're obviously ready for bed. We can talk tomorrow—'

'I'm leaving in the morning for the Dordogne—'

'I know. Tabby did mention how close I'd come to

missing you,' Andreo interposed evenly. 'Isn't it fortunate that I have a home in the same region? You'll be able to travel down with me.'

At the mere idea that she might be willing to travel anywhere with him, Pippa breathed in so deep and long that she was almost convinced she would burst.

'Is it OK if I have a shower?' Andreo enquired, setting his case down on the luggage rack by the wall.

'You *can't* sleep here!' Pippa exclaimed, blue eyes huge.

'No problem. Perhaps you'd do the honours with our hostess and request a separate room for me.'

Pippa paled and tried to steel herself to the prospect of rising to that challenge. Tabby would be embarrassed by her assumption that her guests would happily share the same bedroom. Pippa would be embarrassed asking for an arrangement that was the equivalent of a public announcement about the hostile state of her current relationship with Andreo. Colour warming her cheeks, she dropped her head.

'You might as well sleep here tonight. It's a big bed and it's late and Tabby and Christien have probably already gone to bed,' she muttered grudgingly.

As he watched her visibly squirm at the idea of approaching her friend unholy amusement at her discomfiture made Andreo say with exaggerated courtesy, 'I wouldn't dream of it. It's obvious that you're uncomfortable with the idea.'

Pippa snatched in a steadying breath but she was relieved that he had sufficient sensitivity to appreciate how difficult she would find such a situation. 'It's all right. I'll be fine,' she said woodenly.

Andreo shed his jacket and tie, unbuttoned his shirt. He had been so angry when he'd arrived, and he still was, but all of a sudden he just wanted to laugh out loud. He very much doubted that their hosts had gone to bed at eleven at night. It was inconceivable to Andreo that he would allow other people's opinions to influence his behaviour, for he was fearless when it came to pursuing any course in which he knew himself to be in the right. It was evident that Pippa was much more vulnerable and he studied her with keen interest. Covered from head to toe in a shapeless garment that would have looked at home in a coffin, she was scrambling into the bed in extreme haste.

While he stripped with the most shocking lack of self-consciousness and not a decent ounce of the extreme awkwardness that Pippa felt he ought to have been suffering in her presence, she turned her back on him to glare at the wall. But the image of his lithe bronzed masculinity travelled with her as powerfully as if he still stood in front of her. She was furious with herself for being severely tempted to sneakily spy on him while he undressed. After all she had said and done, what sort of sense would that make?

But then was there any sense at all to what was happening between them now? Suppose he was telling her the truth about Lili Richards? Why, after all, would he follow her all the way to France if she had only been the two-week equivalent of a one-night stand? Maybe he had been planning to visit the country anyway: he did own a house in France, she reminded herself.

She lay in bed, tossing and turning, listening with one ear to the distant sound of the shower running in the connecting bathroom. It shook her that she couldn't get her thoughts into any kind of reasonable order. She was in total turmoil. In search of an explanation, she looked back to the outset of their affair...

She had spent ten consecutive days with Andreo D'Alessio. Only work hours had intervened and they had soon alleviated that problem by stealing at least two hours together around midday. In retrospect she was shocked at the feckless attitudes she had fallen into. Andreo had wanted her and that had been that: she couldn't have cared less about Venstar. For the entirety of those ten days she had lived entirely for Andreo. They had not spent a single night apart. The one evening on which she had suggested that she ought to go home, Andreo had wasted no time in dissuading her from the notion.

Never before had she been so indescribably happy. That reality spoke for itself, her more sober self interposed at that point. Happiness of that magnitude was not meant to last and once she had tasted the best she should have known that it could only get worse from there on in. How much worse? Andreo was an unrepentant womaniser...and there was a possibility that she might be expecting his baby!

No, no, *no*! Pippa shrieked inside her mind, fighting to throw that scary thought back out again. The chances of her being pregnant were very small, she told herself doggedly. If her cycle did not return to normal soon, she would consider approaching a doctor. A little voice she did not want to listen to reminded her that her own mother might only have conceived once but that conception had actually taken place when her parents had only been together for two short weeks!

Andreo sauntered out of the bathroom. All that stood between him and total nudity was a pair of seriously trendy Armani boxers. Pippa stared. She preferred distracting herself to suffering what she regarded as almost hysterical fears relating to pregnancy, or almost as bad, succumbing to a need to mentally dissect every blasted minute she had ever spent in his company. Her mesmerised attention roamed over the hard contours of his strong, muscular shoulders, broad, powerful chest, the flat slab of his stomach and long, strong thighs. Lean muscle rippled in the smooth bronze expanse of his back and narrow hips as he closed his case and straightened, a magnificent male animal in his athletic and sexual prime. The tip of her tongue slunk out to moisten her dry lower lip. She was conscious of the heated, heavy rise of excitement low in her pelvis, the aching pulse of moist responsive heat.

'No…' Andreo said softly.

Her reactions slowed by her distance from rational thought, Pippa blinked and focused on him. 'Sorry?'

'I'm off limits. You would have to get down on your knees and beg before I would forgive you for your behaviour—'

'Off limits?' Pippa was unable to credit her own hearing. 'Get down on my knees and beg? What for?'

'Sex…sex with me, *amore*.' Andreo tossed back the sheet and came down beside her, black hair tousled, stunning dark golden eyes burnished to sizzling gold. 'Don't think I don't know when you want me—'

Pippa turned the same colour as a ripe beetroot, yanked up a pillow and tried to thump him with it. 'That's utter nonsense!'

'And how violent you can be when you don't get it.' Removing the pillow from her fevered grasp, Andreo tossed it behind his head and stretched with the flexing, fluid grace of a prowling tiger. Angling a knowing appraisal at her, he smiled with unholy complacency.

In one furious jerk, Pippa sat up. 'You know nothing about me—'

'I know you kept *every* single flower and card I ever sent you, even the dying blooms,' Andreo commented smooth as silk.

'So what?' she raked at him. 'I hate waste!'

'Tabby said you had been inconsolable since your arrival but trying hard to cover it up,' Andreo added.

Ready to claw like a wildcat, Pippa launched herself at him and hissed scornfully, 'There's no way Tabby would say something like that to you...she's my friend!'

Andreo took advantage of her proximity to close strong hands round her forearms and tip her down on top of him.

Sudden silence fell. Her hands had come down on his chest to steady herself, slender fingers spreading on warm, hair-roughened muscles. Her breath caught in her throat. When her startled blue eyes collided with his burning gold scrutiny, the atmosphere was electric and the fight and the anger went out of her as surely as if he had pulled a switch.

Andreo meshed a lean-fingered hand in the tumble of her cinnamon-coloured curls and stole one devastating, passionate kiss. Breathing shallowly, he freed her reddened mouth again and lifted her back onto her own side of the bed.

Excitement had seethed up in a tempestuous greedy burst inside Pippa. Her body was clamouring for the satisfaction that he had taught her to want. She rolled over, and like an iron filing drawn by a magnet, reached for him again. But Andreo dealt her a smouldering look and set her back from him in unashamed rejection. 'I'm still too angry with you...'

'Angry?' she repeated, aghast and in shock from what had just happened.

Andreo settled grim dark golden eyes on her. 'If I ever

want someone else, I will tell you up front. That's how I am. I don't lie or sneak around. I don't need to. To date there may have been a fair number of women in my life but none could ever accuse me of dishonesty or infidelity, *cara*.'

'Lili Richards touched you...*that* was infidelity!' Pippa slammed back in a ferocious surge of disagreement. 'One finger on any part of you qualifies as infidelity!'

Andreo screened his amused gaze. 'Is that a fact? I don't like being pawed in public. I think it's tasteless. Presumably you didn't see me push her away and ask her to cool it—'

'No, I didn't. And before you come over all smug and think that you broke my heart and that that's why I left London, think again!' Pippa hauled up the sheet and turned her slim, elegant back on him. 'Our relationship had run its course and it was time for it to end. I decided to go to France right at the *start* of our affair and I never once swerved from that decision!'

During the blistering silence that fell in answer to that declaration, hot stinging tears inched out from below Pippa's lowered eyelids and slid down her cheeks onto the pillow. She knew she would not be able to sleep by his side.

CHAPTER EIGHT

HAVING lain awake for half the night, Pippa drifted off around seven and woke with a start an hour later. Her nostrils flared on the rich, aromatic smell of fresh coffee and her stomach instantly rebelled. Eyes flying wide in dismay, she threw herself off the bed, hurtled past Andreo where he stood with a laden breakfast tray and raced at all possible speed into the bathroom. She was sick but, mercifully, it was over quickly and she felt fine in the aftermath.

'Are you OK?' Andreo enquired from the doorway.

Her embarrassment intense, Pippa stalked across the bathroom and slammed shut the door in his face, snapping, 'Can't I even be ill in peace?'

After a lengthy shower, an even slower drying-off of her curls into fluffy childish bangs that infuriated her, she emerged and found the bedroom empty, which, oddly enough, annoyed her even more than a barrage of questions would have done. When she went downstairs, Tabby took her into the dining room for breakfast.

'Andreo said you weren't well. He's worried about you…he's a real hunk too, isn't he?' Tabby lowered her voice to add with an irreverent grin. 'Christien gets on with him like a house on fire.'

'I could have forecast that without a crystal ball,' Pippa confided. 'Where are they?'

'Well, they made a great play about going off to talk business…but I bet you anything that they'll end up either down in the wine cellar or having a spin in

Christien's latest new car,' Tabby declared with her warm, contagious laugh.

'What's the fastest way of finding out if you're pregnant?' Pippa asked her friend in a rush.

Tabby blinked and breathed in deep and let the silence linger before saying, 'I could take you to see my doctor. He'll do a test.'

Tabby made the necessary phone call while Pippa sipped at a cup of tea but only shredded a piece of toast for she was too nervous to feel hungry. As they walked out to Tabby's car her friend gave her a rueful appraisal. 'Thanks for trusting me.'

'Terror loves company,' Pippa quipped half under her breath.

An hour later, she knew for sure: she was going to have a baby. No longer could she hide her head in the sand and hope that only nerves were upsetting her system. But she was shattered by that confirmation.

'What are you planning to do?' Tabby asked her friend worriedly during the drive back to the château.

'I don't know,' Pippa confided unevenly, and it was the truth.

She had had such an unhappy childhood and she had only to picture some poor child suffering in a similar way for her heart to sink. Of course, she knew that she would never punish a child for poor academic performance. She would not comment on her child's lack of good looks either. Nor would she ever tell her son or her daughter as her mother had once told her that she was only staying in a bad, destructive relationship for *their* sake.

'Talk it over with Andreo...he *is*...I mean...the baby is his?' Tabby gave her friend an apologetic look.

Pippa nodded in rueful confirmation.

'He's fabulous with kids,' Tabby informed her eagerly.

'Jake and Jolie climbed all over him this morning and he was very good-natured about it. You've just been taken by surprise, Pippa. You'll get used to the idea.'

'I'm sure I will…' The very concept of accepting that new life was growing inside her shook Pippa deeply. It seemed so extraordinary, almost a miracle, something worthy of celebration rather than fear and anxiety.

'I adore babies,' Tabby admitted, bringing her car to a halt outside her huge imposing home and switching off the engine. 'Christien thought we should wait until Jolie was older but I didn't want to. I prefer not to have big age gaps between our children.'

Christien and Andreo strode out through the front entrance to greet them.

One glimpse of Andreo's riveting dark features and Pippa's heart skipped a beat. Casually clad in an aqua short-sleeved shirt and beige chinos, he looked heart-stoppingly handsome She thought of how she had planned to tell him that she was already booked on a train to the Dordogne and abandoned the idea. Now that she knew about the baby, Andreo would have to be told as well. And perhaps, she thought unhappily, it was time she stopped trying to tell herself that she would be able to walk away from him without pain, for that was an outright lie.

'You didn't say you were going out, *ma belle*,' Christien said to his wife, lean strong face reproving.

'You didn't say you were taking Andreo out for a spin round the estate in the McLaren…or did I miss that announcement?' his wife fielded cheekily.

Andreo decided to take advantage of their audience and Pippa's unusually timid aspect, for her bright blue eyes had yet to meet his. 'Your luggage is already on board the helicopter.'

Involuntarily, Pippa experienced a moment of amusement. He had not been able to kidnap her but he had kidnapped her luggage and her diary. Little more than ten minutes later, their farewells exchanged, they were walking towards the helipad.

'How are you feeling?'

'Great...this morning was just one of those things,' she dismissed hurriedly. 'Where's this property of yours in the Dordogne?'

'Near Bourdeilles. The countryside around there reminded me of Tuscany,' he volunteered. 'Unspoilt farmland and woods. You'll like my house. It's very relaxing.'

'I'm sure it is, but I'll be taking a room in Brantome...my mother is buried near there,' she responded brittly. 'This is my first trip back to France since I was seventeen and something of a pilgrimage. There was a car crash that summer and my mother and several of my parents' friends died. If I stayed with you, you wouldn't find me good company.'

Andreo had read about the accident in the investigation report. Having spoken to his pilot, he watched her struggle to do up her seat belt and intervened to do it for her. Her pale, delicate profile was taut, the tension in her slender body as pronounced as that etched in the unusual clumsiness of her hands.

They landed at a private airfield and continued their journey in the Mercedes four-wheel drive that awaited them. The landscape was becoming familiar to her and she was silent. Haunted by painful memories of that fatal summer, she finally closed her eyes and drifted off to sleep.

'We're here...'

When Andreo wakened Pippa, she could not recall ever having slept more heavily. She clambered out of the car in as much of a daze as a sleepwalker. Having simply assumed that Andreo was planning to drop her off in the centre of Brantome, she was disconcerted to find herself standing instead outside a small rural church.

'I remembered the details from the investigation report.' Andreo reached into the car boot and lifted out a beautiful bouquet of fresh flowers. 'I stopped off in a village on the way for these but I should have woken you up so that you could choose—'

'No, they're lovely.' Her voice wobbled, for she was touched by his kindness and suddenly very grateful indeed not to be alone.

Andreo curved a strong arm to her spine because even in the warmth of the sunshine she was trembling. It did not take them long to find what they sought in the beautifully kept graveyard. She knelt down and gently laid the flowers on the springy turf and struggled to maintain control over her unsettled emotions.

'That summer we were staying in a village only a stone's throw from here. It was a disastrous, horrible holiday,' she confided, the words tumbling from her in an enervated torrent. 'Tabby was all tied up with Christien and her ghastly stepmother, Lisa, was flirting like mad with my dad. He loved all the attention. I had a fight with Mum on the day of the accident. I told her we should go home and leave Dad free to flirt with Lisa and Mum was mad with me…and I said I was ashamed of her because she let Dad treat her like dirt!' A sob was wrenched from Pippa. 'We made up but I should never have spoken to her like that.'

Andreo rested level dark golden eyes on her distraught face. 'She was your mother. She would have understood, *cara mia*.'

But Pippa could not stop the tears falling, for she had

never come to terms with the terrible costs of that crash or the frightening emotional turmoil into which she had been cast in its aftermath. How could she ever have forgiven herself for wishing even momentarily that it had been her mother and not her father who had survived? For hating her father for insisting that she could not be spared from his bedside to travel to her own mother's funeral? Andreo just held her close and let her cry.

'OK...' Recognising when the storm was over, Andreo assisted her back into the Mercedes.

Pippa felt drained and yet curiously at peace as well. For the first time she noticed that it was a seriously beautiful day, and while Andreo was driving through the town she told him about her infatuation with Pete and subsequent disillusionment. 'Men always did go for Tabby in a big way,' she completed with an accepting shrug of her shoulders.

'She lacks your elegance,' Andreo drawled. 'He had no taste.'

The Mercedes purred through sleepy Gascon villages lined with ancient stone houses. She had forgotten how lovely the lush green landscape was in early summer. The little town of Bordeilles was on the River Dronne and she could remember visiting the tall dignified château that towered over the other buildings.

'Aren't you going the wrong way?' she murmured.

'I'm taking you home with me, *amore*.'

'I should argue but I can't be bothered.' But she knew even as she said it that she was talking nonsense, making excuses sooner than admit that wild horses could not have torn her from his side. She just needed to be with him and she refused to question why that was. A couple of kilometres beyond the town he swung off the road and into a dusty laneway where he paused and lowered the window.

'That's it over there...'

She looked across a field of yellow black-eyed sunflowers to see the building with the tower that sat on the far side of it. Fashioned of the local honey-coloured stone and roofed with warm reddish-brown tiles, the house looked as if it had stood in that precise spot for ever.

'How old is it?' she asked as he drove on down the lane.

'Fourteenth century. It was a priory and it holds a special place in my heart. I bought it when I was eighteen—'

'*Eighteen?*' she gasped, sitting up out of her slump.

'I ran away from home because my family persisted in treating me like a teenager—'

'You *were* a teenager at eighteen—'

Andreo gave her a mocking glance. 'We'll talk about my misspent youth some other time.'

He drew up in the deep shade of a grove of stately chestnut trees. At the foot of the hill, a slow-moving river wound through a meadow. There was a stillness that she could literally hear. Drenched in late afternoon sunshine, the house drew her out of the car and the shadows. She roved ahead of him to where the ancient studded wooden door already stood wide in welcome on a hall painted a deep blue as intense as the sky.

'Blue...'

'My favourite colour,' Andreo breathed huskily from behind her. 'Just like your eyes.'

If I didn't already love him, Pippa reflected helplessly, I would love him now for talking nonsense and owning this glorious house. 'Is there someone else here?'

'I asked my housekeeper to air it, stock up for my

arrival and then go home again,' Andreo confided. 'She lives only a couple of fields away.'

'You plan everything, don't you?'

'Don't you?'

She was surprised by that comeback, even more surprised to acknowledge that he was right. She did plan virtually everything in her life. Only she hadn't planned on him or the baby. Once more she thought of the baby as the tiny new life force it was: part of him, part of her, an individual created between them and dependent on them both. Her throat thickened. Slowly she turned to face him, blue eyes softening as she let her admiring attention rest on his breathtakingly handsome features. If their baby was a boy, he would be very handsome, and if their baby was a girl, she hoped she inherited her blue eyes and Andreo's gorgeous black hair.

'You'll stay, *cara*?'

With difficulty she shook free of her sentimental little daydream and focused on him. He was temptation personified to her. 'But only—'

Andreo placed a reproachful forefinger briefly against her full pink lower lip. 'No boundaries,' he warned her lazily. 'I don't like boundaries.'

'I need them.'

'You have to trust me.'

She felt like glass he could see through: naked and vulnerable. He had cut through her intended protests to the heart of the matter. An issue of trust. He might as well have asked her to scale Everest barefoot, she thought in dismay. She did not think that she had it in her to truly trust a male of his calibre. He was far too rich and good-looking. *Not* his fault, she conceded painfully. Nature had blessed him with lean, dark, devastating features and an incredibly powerful sexual aura. He had become a target

for women and had learnt to appreciate the extent of his
own power. But wasn't she going to have to trust him
again to tell him about the baby she carried? How could
she expect more from him than she was prepared to give
herself?

'No boundaries,' Andreo repeated softly, closing a lean
strong hand over hers and leading her up the wide stone
staircase to the upper floor.

In the bedroom, her attention was stolen by the mas-
sive arched window that looked right out over the river
valley. The view was spectacular and the light so strong
that it hurt her eyes with its brilliance. Coming to a halt
behind her, Andreo ran down the zip on her dress and
lingered to press his lips to the soft, sensitive spot where
her neck met the slope of her shoulder.

The unbearably delicious sensation made her squirm
in his hold and with a helpless gasp she let her head fall
back. He skimmed the light dress down over her arms
and she curved her hands down to ensure the fabric did
not catch and linger at her wrists.

'I'm shameless,' she muttered, taken aback by her own
collusion.

Andreo uttered a husky laugh. 'I *wish*...'

Pippa tensed, eyes wide and vulnerable. 'Do you?'

'Only teasing, *amore*. I like you just as you are which
means that you have to resist every other guy around but
be a complete pushover for me,' Andreo confided as he
spun her round in his arms.

Her heart was pounding like crazy. He bent down,
swept her up with an easy masculine strength that was
incredibly seductive and tumbled her down onto the cool
quilted spread.

Pippa surveyed him with sudden shaken intensity as if

she couldn't quite work out how she had ended up there. 'I shouldn't be doing this—'

'That's what you like about me…I send you off the rails, *amore*.'

'And where do you get that idea?'

'You don't take risks…you're the lady with the colour-coded wardrobe, the books in alphabetical order, the tidiest desk. But you took a risk on me.' A vibrant smile that made her heart flip slashed his lean, powerful face.

'I want my diary back,' she told him unsteadily.

Andreo laughed. 'You know I won't read it. Last night was payback time and I enjoyed making you dance to my tune. But don't *ever* walk out on me again without telling me that you're leaving.'

Something in his intonation chilled her. He wasn't laughing any more; he was warning her. But I'm not back with you again, her conscience urged her to tell him. Only how could she tell him what she was doing with him when she didn't know herself? She had made a choice without even being aware of it. She was lying half naked on his bed in his house and, for the first time in countless days of suffocating unhappiness, she felt alive again.

'Kiss me…' she muttered unevenly.

Smouldering golden eyes raked over her slender figure, lingering on the delicate swell of her breasts above the dainty cups of her white bra and the lithe shapely length of slender thighs bisected by white high cut briefs. He pulled his designer shirt over his head and tossed it aside with unashamed eagerness. She lay there looking up at him, feeling her straining nipples pinch tight while a wanton little frisson of heat slivered up from deep within her pelvis.

'You're so beautiful I can't keep my hands off you.'

Magnificent torso bronzed and bare, Andreo lifted her up to him. She was already melting like ice-cream in the hot sun from outside in. And then he claimed her mouth with shattering carnality, penetrating between her readily parted lips with the rhythmic erotic timing of an expert lover. Instantly she caught fire, breathing in gasping shallow spurts, coming back to him again and again for more of the same. Deftly, he discarded her bra. One hand at her spine, he crushed her tender rose-tipped breasts against the hard wall of his muscular chest. Rising on her knees, liquid heat thrumming through her, she pushed even closer to find his passionate mouth again for herself.

'I want you now, *amore*,' Andreo growled thickly, pressing her back onto the bed with a sudden masculine mastery that thrilled her and hooking lean, impatient fingers into her panties to peel them off.

She lay there, hot and quivering and aching for him. She was shamelessly aware of her own readiness, of the moist secret heat that had begun gathering even before his first kiss.

He unzipped his chinos, shedding them and his boxers in a careless heap. Her breath caught in her throat at the extent of his bold arousal.

'I don't want to wait,' he murmured raggedly, staring down into her blushing face, drawn by the glow of desire and appreciation she could not hide.

Passion-glazed eyes locked to him, she angled back her hips and parted her thighs in a sudden provocative move that shocked him almost as much as it shocked her. With a ground-out Italian imprecation and his golden eyes ablaze he came down to her, a raw, fierce need stamped on his startlingly handsome face that made her body thrum with wanton anticipation. He sank into her, deep and strong and without ceremony. Like hitching a ride on a rocket, it was the most exciting event of her life. For the first time she sensed that he was no longer in control and that made her own hunger climb even higher.

'Andreo,' she framed, not even aware that she was sobbing out his name.

The sound of that urgent cry drove him on. He plunged into her faster and faster. Lost in the mindless pleasure of his pagan possession, she moved against him, frantic, fevered, abandoned in her encouragement and welcome. Her heart was racing so hard and fast she was convinced she was flying. Raw excitement sent her spiralling into a wild climax. An uncontrollable frenzy of pleasure gripped her in wave after wave of ecstasy and she writhed under him. With an uninhibited shout of satisfaction, he shuddered over her in a white-hot release that surpassed anything he had ever felt and subsided.

Pippa floated back to planet earth to find that she had both arms possessively wound round Andreo in a way that would never qualify as cool. He rolled over, kissed her breathless and kept her clamped to him with a strong arm.

'Sleep, *amore*,' he urged.

She studied him. His black lashes accentuated the tough angles of his hard, smooth cheekbones, wide strong mouth and stubborn jaw-line. He had a classic masculine profile and he was totally, absolutely gorgeous. She pushed her face into a muscular brown shoulder and breathed in the aroma of his skin with an addict's intensity.

'You can have your diary back,' he muttered with a husky sound of amusement. 'You just settled your debt for all time. That was *amazing*…'

She stayed close, for every tiny moment with him felt

unbearably precious and she was convinced that telling him that she was pregnant would destroy what they had. Reality would dispel the magic. Instantly she would become the reverse of sexy and fanciable, she thought with pained regret. Instead she would become a problem: a woman with the right to decide whether or not he became a father. It was a choice he got no say in and a situation he could surely only resent. After all, he had not been careless; he had taken all possible precautions to try and ensure that she did not conceive. But fate had decided otherwise.

In truth she was in no hurry to admit that she was carrying his child, for she already knew that she would not seek a termination. She herself had been conceived outside marriage and her mother had acknowledged her right to life, so how could she do less for her own baby?

She loved Andreo and that too had to influence her feelings towards his child. Indeed she had begun to love him within minutes of meeting him. But he was not in love with her and theirs was a casual affair. A fling, frothy and fun, nothing serious, she told herself sternly, suppressing her pain at the threat of the inevitable parting ahead. How long would they have together in France? She feared that the idyll would end the instant she confessed to being pregnant.

'So amazing,' Andreo continued thoughtfully, 'That it is time to come clean—'

She tensed. 'About what?'

'Last night you said that you made plans to come to France after we met and never wavered from that goal,' he reminded her. 'That *must* have been a lie.'

Of course it had been a lie. But in the space of a heartbeat she could picture how trapped he might feel if she were to reveal that she loved him and follow that up with an announcement that she was pregnant. He would feel trapped and she would feel humiliated. Why should she sacrifice her pride to that extent? A baby that was the result of an accident in birth control during a casual affair would be rather less disturbing for him than one conceived with a woman who burdened his conscience with the additional news of her undying devotion.

'You only said it because you weren't ready to admit that all that fierce and very flattering jealousy of yours over Lili was quite unnecessary,' Andreo breathed with lethal conviction. 'I am a straightforward guy in relationships—'

'Perhaps you are, but I was only being honest,' Pippa swore in an uneasy undertone against his shoulder. 'We had a fantastic time in London but these things don't last…'

Long fingers speared into her riotous curls and lifted her head. Burnished golden eyes struck hers in a sparking collision course that made the breath catch in her throat. 'And how would a woman who has never known any other lover *know* that for a fact?' he intoned very soft and low and his accent thick on every syllable.

Her gaze veiled to hide her pain and her colour receded. 'I just knew—'

Andreo tumbled her off him and moved with disconcerting speed and dexterity to pin her under him instead. 'So I give you great sex and nothing else?'

Her face flamed and shamed embarrassment at the depths that pretence had reduced her to made her steal an unwise upward glance. She was ensnared by hot golden eyes as aggressive as an invasion force. 'Well…er—'

Andreo flashed her a scorching smile that was extremely unsettling. 'To think I wasted all that effort on soppy flowers and sentimental cards—'

'No, I really *liked*—'

'No need to pretend, *cara*.' Lithe as a jungle cat, Andreo shifted and settled between her thighs with an erotic expertise that made her heart jump inside her.

He kissed her with passionate force. She quivered, fought to concentrate, knowing she should argue in her own defence. He kissed her again and her thoughts blurred while she burned and she ached all over again for a satisfaction he had given her only minutes earlier. She blushed fierily for her own weakness. 'Andreo—?'

'Want me?' he prompted thickly, an irresistible gleam of sexy challenge in his molten gaze.

And she did, oh, how she wanted him: more than pride or common sense or reason. On every level all that was feminine in her responded to his raw masculinity and she could not fight her own nature. And on that liberating reflection, she surrendered to his passion.

Five glorious days later Pippa woke up to find herself alone, but there was nothing new in that for Andreo always got up first.

Her tummy felt queasy and, with a rueful grimace over the awareness that only Andreo's preference for rising with the dawn had protected her from having her secret exposed, she rolled off the bed and headed into the bathroom. But, as had happened the morning before, that initial nausea slowly receded again. Perhaps the worst of her sickness was already over, she thought cheerfully and, pulling on a light cotton wrap, she went downstairs in search of Andreo. Both he and the Mercedes were nowhere to be found, however, and a note left on the hall

table informed her that he had gone out to buy chocolate
croissants for her.

An ear to ear smile curved her lips.. He was spoiling
her again and she had already discovered that she absolutely adored every moment of being spoilt. She had
never been a self-indulgent woman or a woman who had
ever imagined that any male might put himself out on
her behalf. Indeed her father's unfortunate example had
persuaded her that all men were instinctively selfish. So
for that reason the sheer amount of effort that Andreo
was prepared to expend on any gesture likely to please
her continually shook her.

'I like surprising you…I enjoy seeing you smile,
amore,' he had confided with the charismatic grin that
made her heart spin inside her.

Eyes dreamy and soft over that memory, Pippa went
for a shower and tried to work out without success how
five whole days had passed at such speed. Why was it
that happy times seemed to shoot past faster than the
speed of light and unhappier times dragged? Brow furrowing on that conundrum, she was on far too much of
an emotional high to linger on it.

While she was in the act of shampooing her hair, her
attention fell on the sunken bath that was set in a glorious
multi-coloured mosaic surround and her skin warmed and
her smile grew abstracted: when they shared the bath they
fooled around like kids. He had taught her how to relax
and overcome her innate fear of making a fool of herself.
He had made her laugh and, over and over again, he had
given her the kind of joy she had never dreamt she might
experience in a hundred years.

She loved the long evenings the most. When the shadows had begun to lengthen and the heat of the day had
ebbed, they would dine at the stone table overlooking the

river and sit talking far into the night. Even the food they were eating was wonderful. Berthe, Andreo's friendly housekeeper, who worked as an occasional chef in her son-in-law's restaurant, performed gastronomic miracles in the kitchen.

Pippa was combing her hair when she thought that she heard the Mercedes return. However, when she ran to the window she could only see Berthe's husband, Guillaume, who farmed Andreo's land, driving a tractor into a field next to the lane. The phone by the bed rang and she answered it.

'It's Tabby,' her friend said cheerfully. 'I've been try-ing to raise you on your mobile—'

'It's dead,' Pippa admitted apologetically. 'I forgot to charge it—'

'Luckily, Christien asked Andreo for his number,' Tabby explained. 'I was really surprised when you didn't phone me—'

'I know,' Pippa groaned, full of squirming guilt. 'I know I should have phoned you—'

Tabby was not slow to take advantage of her friend's discomfiture. 'So stop holding out on me and tell me what's happening between you two.'

When a noisy click sounded on the line, Pippa as-sumed they had a bad connection and raised her voice to be heard over the interference. 'There's really nothing to tell—'

'Does that mean that you *still* haven't told him about the baby?' Tabby exclaimed in a tone of disbelief.

'Tabby...' Pippa felt stabbed in the back by that in-credulity. After all, what harm was she doing in remain-ing silent a little longer?

'I wouldn't have asked if I hadn't found you in resi-dence at the end of Andreo's phone line,' Tabby sighed, sounding even more anxious. 'I'm sorry…forget I even mentioned the baby. I really didn't mean to put pressure on you. It's just…I've been *so* worried.'

But Pippa's attention had been stolen from their conversation for she had heard a step on the stone stairs. She spun round just as Andreo appeared in the arched doorway. Sheathed in faded denim jeans and a black designer shirt, he looked darkly handsome and dangerous. When she clashed with the furious challenge in his hard appraisal, she frowned in bewilderment and then gulped at the sight of the cordless phone grasped in his hand. From that phone Tabby's voice could still be clearly heard setting up an echo in concert with the phone that Pippa held herself. Her blood ran cold: Andreo must have lifted the phone downstairs and overheard their dialogue.

'Sorry, I have to go…' Pippa breathed flatly. 'I'll call you later.'

CHAPTER NINE

'I ASSUMED you were still in bed. I lifted the hall phone to call Marco. Is it true?' Andreo demanded.

Pippa was very pale but reluctant to accept that he knew her secret. 'Is what true?'

Andreo dealt her a raw look of derision. 'Is it true that you're pregnant?'

Pippa breathed in slow and deep to steady herself and laced her hands together in a nervous motion. 'Yes...'

'And is the baby mine?'

She reddened. 'How can you ask me a question like that?'

'Easily. This is not how I expected to hear that kind of news from you. Since it's clear you're not the very honest woman I thought you were, what else might I have got wrong?' Andreo fielded harshly, lean, strong face rigid with the same tension that was holding her taut.

'Not that anyway...the baby *is* yours,' she stated in driven reproach.

Stunning golden eyes veiling, Andreo swung away from her so that she could not see how he had taken that blunt confirmation of his paternity.

Had he had some wild hope that he might not be the male responsible for impregnating her? Pippa wondered in dismay. She felt demeaned by that suspicion but could not avoid thinking along such lines. He had taken her to bed. At no time had he talked of a future that lay further away than the next day. Those were the facts. Facts that were bare of the taint of her hopes and dreams. Naturally

Andreo would have been relieved to hear that the responsibility for the baby she carried was not his.

'This is not the way I wanted you to find out about my…er…condition,' Pippa muttered uncomfortably, shying away from that word, 'baby', lest it increase his shock.

'Don't try to fool me. You had no plans to tell me at all. Why else would you have remained silent this long? Do you think I haven't worked that out for myself?' It was a low, bitter response that sliced through the tense atmosphere like a knife blade.

'I don't know what you're trying to say…' Pippa could hardly think straight because she felt wretched. Last night and every night since her arrival at his idyllic home in the Dordogne she had slept in his arms, but now he was poised on the far side of the room surveying her with grim, shuttered eyes as though she were his mortal enemy. 'Of course I was going to tell you… OK, so I wasn't in a hurry to do it, but I hardly think that's a crime!'

'*Per meraviglia*…I think you were more concerned that I might try to interfere in how you chose to deal with what you no doubt saw as a colossal problem,' Andreo framed in a raw undertone. 'That's why you left London but you weren't prepared to admit that. If I hadn't heard you talking to Christien's wife, I would never have found out that I'd got you pregnant. You intended to keep that fact from me. Why won't you admit that?'

Pippa stared back at him in consternation. 'Because it's not true and I wouldn't behave like that. You've got it all wrong—'

'I don't think so.' Hard dark eyes assailed hers with fierce distrust.

Andreo was playing judge, jury and executioner all at

one and the same time and very much in his element, Pippa decided in furious frustration. 'You aren't listening to what I'm saying—'

'Why would I?' Andreo vented a derisive laugh. 'Why would I listen to a woman who has so little regard for either me or our relationship that she leaves the country without even leaving me a note?'

'You *know* why that happened!' Pippa protested, alarmed by that condemnation being recycled. 'I saw you with Lili Richards and assumed the worst—'

'As you chose not to confront me on that score, I only have your word for that. In point of fact, you just vanished—'

'My departure from London had nothing to do with me being pregnant because I only found out that I had fallen pregnant the day after you arrived in France!' Pippa argued vehemently, her bright blue eyes pinned to his lean chiselled features with a concern she could not hide. 'I was planning to tell you, I *was*—'

'I don't think so. Your behaviour speaks for itself—'

'And what's that supposed to mean?'

Implacable golden eyes raked over her with stubborn force. 'I think that the moment you discovered that you were rather more fertile than you wanted to be, you decided to walk out on me and go for an abortion. Perhaps you came to France first in an effort to ensure that you shook me off.'

Pippa's back was so rigid her spine was protesting her stance, but her pallor was now illuminated by angry colour. 'You have no right to talk as if you can get inside my head and somehow know what *I* was planning to do—'

Andreo sent her a fierce look of derision. 'I don't need a fortune-teller, do I? You don't like children—'

'That is untrue and what is more I never said any such thing.'

His wide sensual mouth compressed into an even more intransigent line. 'You don't *want* children—'

'What would you know about what I want?' Pippa flung at him hotly. 'Maybe I started to feel differently when I realised I was already carrying a baby.'

Andreo's keen gaze narrowed and glittered. His strong bone structure bearing a little less resemblance to a stone wall, he took a sudden fluid step closer. 'Did you?'

'That's none of your business! You should have asked how I felt...*nicely*, not gone straight into attack!' she snapped back at him.

'Don't tell me it's none of my business when you have my baby inside you!' Andreo thundered back at her.

'When you talk like that you sound like a fourteenth-century man,' she told him with a scornfully curled lip.

His sense of humour nowhere in evidence, Andreo jerked a powerful shoulder in dismissal. 'It's my baby too and I made it clear that I would take full responsibility if this happened.'

'Always supposing I wanted you to take responsibility,' Pippa slotted in, if anything more angry than ever that he should dare to imply that she needed him to take care of her and the baby she carried.

'Any decisions you make should be discussed with me,' Andreo delivered grimly.

'All right.' Pippa forced out a facetious laugh. 'Are you any good at changing nappies?'

Andreo gave her an arrested look.

Pippa released an exaggerated sigh of disappointment. 'Obviously you've no experience whatsoever in that line. What about feeds and crying bouts in the middle of the night?'

His level black brows pleated in a bemused frown. 'We'd have a nanny.'

'Oh, would we?'

'Of course…' But for once Andreo was out of his depth and it was showing in the intensity with which he was watching her while he tried to guess what the right answers might be on her terms. He had half a dozen nephews and nieces but he had had precious little to do with them as babies.

'So while you are convinced that you should be involved in any decisions I make, you're not actually willing to do any hands-on parenting—'

'What is this conversation? Are you saying that you *are* prepared to have this baby if I get involved?' Andreo demanded tautly.

'If you had ever taken the time to ask me, I would have told you up front that I had already decided that I was going to have this child.' Pippa was breathing in slowly and carefully because the sheer stress of their confrontation was making her head swim. 'But I don't need you or your money to manage and if a nanny is all you have to offer, I think we might just be better off on our own.'

'That's *not* all I'm prepared to offer,' Andreo breathed with savage clarity, brilliant eyes shimmering over her. 'I'll marry you…obviously.'

Pippa almost flinched from the demeaning form that that proposal took and a great hollowness entered her then, for it hurt her a great deal that he could even think that she would consider allowing him to marry her. Marriage was for people who couldn't bear to live apart and who wanted to make a proper commitment to each other. Occasionally people did enter marriage for more prosaic reasons, but she had too much intelligence and way too much pride to become part of such an unequal union: he didn't love her and that was that. Therefore there was nothing to discuss. As far as she was concerned, how much she loved him did not enter the equation. Nobody knew better than she how disastrous such a marriage could be.

'You need me in bed *and* out of it, *cara mia*,' Andreo asserted with ferocious assurance. 'I want you and I want our child as well.'

Hot tears prickled at the back of Pippa's eyes but she held them back. She would not look at him because she could not bear to betray the utter turmoil of her emotions. Brushing past him before he could even guess her intention, she headed downstairs and reached for the phone book.

'I'm going to call a cab. What's the address here?' she asked Andreo where he lowered like a dark, threatening storm at the foot of the stone staircase.

'You can't leave—'

'Watch me!' But her defiant glance in his direction fell short for his image was blurring because she was feeling horribly giddy.

'I asked you to marry me,' Andreo ground out with chilling hauteur.

'Gosh, *did* you?' Pippa sniped back in response, fighting off the dizziness assailing her with all her might. 'How did I miss that? I heard you tell me with great condescension that you would marry me and that I needed you. Well, listen well, I don't *need* anybody but myself!'

With feverish haste, she headed back upstairs but on the first step a hand came down over hers where it rested on the balustrade and effectively arrested her progress. 'This is incredibly childish,' Andreo asserted.

'You said it…' Pippa was desperate to make her escape before she broke down and cried her eyes out.

'I will not chase round France after you,' Andreo breathed in a warning growl.

'I don't want you to chase after me.' Her skin felt horribly clammy and her tummy was rolling with nausea. With a supreme effort, she dragged her hand free of his restraint and blindly mounted another step.

'I think that you do but this time it's not going to happen. You've done everything you can to undermine our relationship and if the proposal didn't come up to scratch, you've only got yourself to thank for it,' Andreo delivered with harsh emphasis. 'You tell me you don't need anyone. At least admit the truth…you're too much of a coward to give me or what we have a chance!'

For a bare instant, Pippa considered that frightening condemnation but her mind was in a state of flux and by that point she was so giddy that she was swaying where she stood. Still struggling to triumph over her light head, she was sucked down a long, suffocating tunnel into the darkness of unconsciousness.

When she surfaced from her faint she was lying down and no sooner had she attempted to lift her head than the nausea returned with cruel strength. Handling that bout of sickness with infuriating efficiency, Andreo carried her back to the bed and told her not to move while he was downstairs.

He reappeared a few minutes later.

Enraged by her own demeaning bodily weakness, Pippa bit out grittily, 'I'm still leaving.'

'If the doctor agrees…' Andreo murmured in the mildest of tones.

'What doctor?'

'The one I've called out. You were very sick.'

'That was just that stupid morning sickness on my stupid empty stomach!' she hissed at him. 'And until you started arguing with me, I was getting over that!'

Andreo continued to survey her with immense calm and cool.

'Stop looking at me like that!' Pippa launched at him wildly. 'Like I'm a kid having a shocking temper tantrum!'

His glorious golden eyes took immediate cover below the dense flourish of his lush black lashes. He said nothing, nothing at all, and while the silence stretched Pippa squirmed on a torture rack of her own making. He had been exceedingly kind and he had not bolted from a situation that the average male avoided like the plague. He might be drop dead gorgeous but he was also amazingly practical. He very probably *could* handle the less rewarding aspects of baby care, she reflected guiltily. Feeling far too emotional and utterly raging at the maddening tears that came to her eyes all too readily, she flipped over on her side and hid under her bright tumbled hair.

'I don't want you to be upset like this,' Andreo murmured levelly from the foot of the bed, resisting a very powerful urge to offer more physical comfort.

'I'm not upset,' she mumbled.

'I was lying when I said I wouldn't chase round France after you, *carissima*,' Andreo imparted silkily.

'Oh…?' Low though she felt it would be to reach for a proffered olive branch, she discovered that she was eager to mend the breach between them.

'I won't let you go free to get lost again,' he spelt out with the lethally quiet diction of a very confident personality. 'You seem to think that there's something wrong with needing me…but all of us need someone and you don't appear to have anyone else.'

At that unexpected speech, Pippa tried and failed to swallow the thickness in her throat. She felt as though she had hit her lowest ebb: he had taken pity on her. What he was doing for her now, he would have done for any woman carrying his child. Essentially he was an honourable guy. Exactly the sort who could be depended on to accept responsibility for an accidental pregnancy. Hence the marriage proposal. She had been right not to listen and to throw that offer back in his face, she told herself wretchedly.

The middle-aged doctor advised her that pregnant ladies required more rest and that keeping the late hours that were presumably responsible for her shadowed eyes was not to be recommended either. It was all common sense stuff. When he had gone, Andreo brought her a delicious lunch on a tray. Her own keen appetite amazed her: she cleared the plate.

'I didn't hear Berthe's car. She really is a fantastic cook.'

'She hasn't arrived yet. I made it...'

Surprise made Pippa exclaim, '*You*...did?'

'Why not? I once lived here alone for six months. Either I learned to look after myself or I went hungry,' Andreo said dryly.

She was feeling incredibly tired and she rested her head down on the pillow. Studying his darkly handsome classic profile, she felt the magnetic pull of his charismatic attraction with every sense she possessed and she could have wept over her own susceptibility. 'Was that when you were eighteen? What were you doing here then?'

'Rebelling, what else?' Andreo rested riveting dark golden eyes on her and vented a rueful laugh. 'I fell in love with a model. Her name was Fia and she was five years older. My father was incapable of waiting for the affair to run its course. He demanded that I give her up and he threatened me with disinheritance in time-honoured style. Fia and I came to France to set up home together. *But*…before I could buy the priory, she accepted a lucrative cash offer from my father to ditch me instead.'

Pippa winced and learned that even though she was inexcusably jealous of any woman he had ever been involved with she still could not bear the idea of him being hurt. And she could well imagine how open and trusting he had been as a teenager.

'I stayed on here to lick my wounds. I wasn't destitute. I had a trust fund from my grandparents. It might not have been sufficient to tempt Fia but it was enough to live on.' His handsome mouth quirked.

He was making light of the hurt he had suffered but she knew him well enough to guess how devastated he would have been by that betrayal. In those days he had been a romantic ready to make sacrifices to be with the woman he loved. The cruellest blow of all for a male of his pride and intelligence must have been the reality that the object of his affections should have proved to be so unworthy, not to mention being fonder of money than she was of him.

'Andreo…' she began, feeling ridiculously tearful again.

'Get some sleep.' Six feet five inches of lean muscular masculinity, he vaulted upright.

'You don't *have* to marry me just because I'm pregnant.'

'I do…you may be very clever but you haven't the survival instincts of a flea,' Andreo informed her equably.

Any desire to be tearful evaporated. Colour flying into

her cheeks, Pippa thrust herself up against the pillows. 'How can you justify saying that?'

'You turn down a job that's yours and abandon a promising career. You run out on a good relationship,' he enumerated without hesitation. 'You're so stubborn you won't even sit down when you're on the brink of fainting. I think that last says it all, *amore*. You may think you can go it alone, but I'm not impressed.'

'When I get up, I'll be feeling well enough to leave,' Pippa asserted tightly, refusing to listen to him. 'I'd be grateful if you'd book a taxi to pick me up here at three.'

Andreo had gone very still. 'No.'

'I intend to have this baby. Right now, that is all you need to know. If I need your help in any way, I'll contact you.' Turning her head away, Pippa hunched under the sheet.

Leaving was the right thing to do, she reminded herself with stubborn determination. If he wanted to take an interest in their baby after the birth, she would allow him to do so. He did not know how lucky he was that she had turned him down. She might have been a gold-digger willing to marry him just to take advantage of his wealth! He was gorgeous, wonderful company and fantastic in bed. Whether he appreciated it or not, her refusal to be impressed by his attack of gallantry was evidence of just how much she loved him. If only they had had another few days together before he had found out that she was pregnant, she reflected miserably.

Andreo tossed something on the bed and her eyes flew open and lodged on her fluffy pink diary. 'I haven't read a word of it,' he assured her.

Pippa flushed and bent her head. 'I know that.'

'I'm supposed to be meeting with my *notaire* this afternoon to discuss the purchase of some land but I'll cancel.'

Pippa did not trust herself to look near him. 'Don't be daft,' she told him with fake casualness. 'All I intend to do is catch up on my sleep while you're out.'

Andreo dropped down into an athletic crouch to establish the visual connection that she was denying him. 'I'll ask Berthe to keep an eye on you...'

'Don't embarrass me like that,' Pippa urged unevenly, bright blue eyes clinging involuntarily to his lean, powerful face.

Andreo reached for her hand. 'OK, but you have to promise to be sensible and sit down at the very first sign of dizziness—'

'OK...'

He bent his arrogant dark head and let his tongue delve provocatively between her lips. He set up a quivering, delicious tightness low in her pelvis. 'You also have to promise to eat everything Berthe puts in front of you—'

'No problem,' she mumbled, tipping up her mouth to the sexy onslaught of his again with all the self-discipline of a rag doll.

'And if you're really good, you get chocolate croissants as an afternoon snack. Get loads and loads of sleep so that I can make passionate love to you when I get back,' he husked between teasing expert kisses that left her literally begging for more, her fingers biting into his forearms. 'But if I still think you're tired, I *won't*...'

Detaching himself from her hold, he strode across the room to pull the shutters closed on the bright morning sunlight. She stared at him and then recalled in sudden dismay that she had not taken a single photo of him since her arrival. 'Hold on...' she urged, panicking at the threat of having to get by in the future without any photos of him.

Andreo watched in astonishment while she scrambled out of bed and dug a camera he had never seen before out of her bag.

'Smile…' she instructed in a slightly wobbly voice and fiddled with the shutters to let in more light.

'You're supposed to be in bed,' Andreo censured.

She caught his smouldering frown for posterity. 'Smile…look normal,' she pleaded.

She managed a handful of shots before she heard Berthe's noisy little car arriving and she got back into bed to rest to please Andreo. As soon as he had gone downstairs, she got up again and furtively packed her case. Conscious that he would probably look in on her before he left to keep his business appointment, she lay down again and was asleep before she knew it.

When she woke up, the bedroom door was just closing and it was almost two in the afternoon. She had slept for almost two hours. Minutes later, she heard the Mercedes engine fire. Andreo was going out and she would not be here when he returned. Like a child she wanted to leap out of bed and watch him drive off and she found it tough to resist that temptation. She stared into space with strained eyes and reminded herself of why, regardless of her love for Andreo, she could not even consider marrying him…

As a teenager, Pippa had learned that her parents' marriage had been a shotgun affair that would never have taken place but for her own unplanned advent into the world. Her father had been a newly qualified teacher when he'd first met the French student working as a language assistant in the same school. For Pippa's mother it had been love at first sight and in later years she had been painfully honest with her daughter in her efforts to excuse her husband's infidelity.

'We only went out together a few times. By the time I realised that I was going to have a child, your father was already dating someone else. He was very popular with the girls and I was too quiet for him, but when I told him that I was pregnant he immediately said that he would marry me,' the older woman had confided. 'It was a huge sacrifice for him and I was grateful.'

But then her mother had had the attitudes of a different generation and had had pitifully few expectations in life. Pippa's mother had clung to the father of her unborn baby and had meekly accepted that he should neither be kind to her nor faithful. Having married a man who did not love her and who indeed resented her, she had paid a heavy price.

That awareness strengthening Pippa's own conviction that she had to leave Andreo before she was tempted into yielding to the strength of her own feelings for him, Pippa pulled on a pale green shift dress and teamed it with a gold linen jacket. The housekeeper, the plump and attractive Berthe, emerged from the kitchen to greet her. The ensuing exchange of pleasantries, voluble on Berthe's side and more strained on Pippa's, was interrupted when the older woman noticed Pippa's suitcase and the conversation took another tack.

Learning that Pippa intended to call a taxi to ferry her into Bourdeilles, Berthe frowned in surprise and then insisted on giving her a lift into the town, explaining that she herself had some shopping to do.

The elderly little Citroën lurched and bounced down the rough lane at alarming speed. Too late did Pippa recall that Andreo had told her that his housekeeper drove as if she were a bat out of hell in a demolition derby.

Reminding herself that the minor road beyond was usually very quiet, Pippa only betrayed her state of nerves with a faint gasp when her companion raked her car straight into a left turn.

The lorry thundering towards them seemed to come round the corner at them out of nowhere. A high-pitched squawk of alarm broke from Berthe as she hauled the steering wheel round in a frantic effort to get out of its path.

I should have married him... was the only thought that animated Pippa's mind and it was a thought that pierced her with literal anguish in the instant that the little car crashed.

CHAPTER TEN

PIPPA opened shaken eyes.

The Citroën was nose down in a ditch. Berthe was sobbing in shock. But neither of them appeared to be hurt and there was no sign of the lorry, which had apparently speeded on past without deigning to notice the car that had almost come to grief below its enormous wheels.

Pippa reached across with an unsteady hand and switched off the car engine. Checking that the older woman was indeed uninjured, she persuaded her that it would be safer to get out of the car. As Pippa clambered out into the dusty ditch the sleeve of her jacket snagged on the wire attached to the fence post that had been torn down by the crash. The fabric ripped and Pippa gritted her teeth as she attempted to free herself without success. Exasperated, she shrugged out of her jacket and, leaving it where it fell, moved with some difficulty over the rough ground to the driver's side to help Berthe.

By the time she had assisted the heavy older woman to climb out of the Citroën, a battered truck containing Berthe's husband, Guillaume, and her strapping son had pulled up beside them. Her relatives had seen the accident from the field across the road where they had been working. Berthe lamented the reality that she had not had a chance to see the registration of the lorry.

Her husband ignored that remark and tucked his wife into his truck as tenderly as if she had been a queen. 'You are safe,' he pointed out, urging Pippa to join the older woman.

'Travel back home with us and I will take you into town in my car instead,' Berthe's son promised Pippa.

'Thank you but I've changed my mind. I don't think I'll go anywhere today.' Pippa's voice emerged a little unevenly but she lifted her head high with an air of decision.

It was amazing how a near brush with mortality could focus the mind, Pippa acknowledged once she had been dropped back to the priory and had managed to convince Berthe and her menfolk that she felt perfectly fine and could safely be left there alone. In fact the sky had never seemed more blue, the sun more golden or the myriad colours of nature's bounty more intense.

How could she have even considered running out on Andreo a second time? She was ashamed of herself and yet curiously excited too by her own daring in choosing to return and lay herself open to the type of hurt that she had always protected herself from. At the same time she was still able to cringe when she remembered Andreo telling her that she was too scared to give him a chance. It was true. Right from the start, she had foreseen the end of their relationship and had sought to make a self-fulfilling prophecy out of her low expectations. At every turn she had undervalued him and what they shared.

Why had it taken her so long to appreciate that Andreo bore not the faintest resemblance to her late father in character? Judging Andreo in the bitter shadow of her parent's infidelity, she had denied the younger man a fair hearing and she had refused to concede him the smallest trust. She had to be more honest with him and the very last thing he deserved was for her to walk out on him again while so much was still unresolved between them.

Twenty minutes later, Andreo drove back from the meeting, which he had cut short, and the first thing he saw was the Citroën upended in the ditch and a woman's jacket lying by the side of the road. Braking to an emergency stop, for his recognition of that garment was instantaneous, he leapt out to check that the car was unoccupied. For an instant he was frozen there and then he flung himself back into the Mercedes and accelerated down the lane.

Waiting to greet him, Pippa hovered in the doorway of the airy salon. The light flooding through the tall, elegant windows behind her burnished her hair with fiery highlights and threw into prominence her taut pallor.

Andreo strode into the hall. Lean, strong face stamped with savage tension, his gaze alight with ferocious strain roved over her in wondering disbelief and shock. '*Per meraviglia!* You're here? Safe and unhurt? When I saw your jacket beside Berthe's car I thought you had been injured…perhaps seriously…and I assumed you had been taken to hospital, only I did not know which one…' At that point, his dark deep drawl thickened and came to a halt.

'We were almost run down by a l-lorry.' Blue eyes welded to his extravagantly handsome features, Pippa was embarrassed by the nervous catch that had crept into her voice. Her heart seemed to pound so frantically inside her chest she could hardly breathe and she found herself gabbling in an almost inaudible rush, 'My mother would have said that an angel must have been in the car with us for Berthe is all in one piece as well…'

Venting a roughened phrase in his own language to best express his disordered emotions, Andreo overcame his paralysis and strode forward to close his arms round her. '*Porca miseria*…if you only knew what I have been thinking!'

Almost immediately he drew back from her again.

Pippa watched him swallow hard and stood without complaint while he ran lean hands down from her shoulders to her hips and studied her with intense concern as though he was not yet able to accept the evidence of his own eyes and credit that she too had escaped injury.

'I got a shock too…Berthe just drove out without looking—'

'You will never, ever get into a car with her again, *amore*,' Andreo intoned harshly, long fingers closing into her shoulders and giving her the tiniest, barely definable shake in emphasis of that embargo.

'She got a terrible fright and I'm sure she'll be much more cautious in the future. I gather the road is usually very quiet—'

He closed one hand into her vibrant mane of curls to tip her head back and scorching golden eyes assailed hers. 'I think if you had died, I would have wanted to die too,' he breathed in a raw, driven undertone. 'You are so much like a part of me now and when you are not with me, I don't feel right. Had I lost you, I should never have felt complete again, *bella mia*.'

Stunned at the extraordinary emotional intensity of that passionate declaration, Pippa stared up at him with parted lips, her amazement palpable. He cared about her, he really, really cared about her. Some of the hard, hurting tension with which she had braced herself to face him began to yield inside her. 'I suppose you've already guessed but I was a-about to take off on you again—'

Dark colour accentuated the sculpted perfection of his masculine cheekbones. '*Sì*…but I was asking for it. I wasn't honest with you. I was still trying to play it cool and of course you needed my reassurance and I had too much pride to let you see how I felt about you…'

Brooding golden eyes veiling below lush black lashes,

Andreo fell frustratingly silent at that point when Pippa was hanging on his every word with superhuman concentration and attention. 'How you feel about…er…me?' she prompted shamelessly.

'I'm working on that,' Andreo assured her between compressed lips, graceful brown hands curving briefly to her cheekbones while he continued to study her and then dropping from her again.

'Oh…' Just for an instant there she had thought he might be about to say he loved her or something crazy like that, and she was really mortified by the fantasy element able to bloom within her own imagination. For the merest instant she wanted to kick him for saying that insane thing about thinking he would have wanted to die had she died. On that score he had undoubtedly led her up the garden path but she was quite sure he had not meant to do so. He had been very much shocked by the sight of that crashed car and he felt very protective towards the baby she carried, and at least she now knew where the Latin reputation for romantic and dramatic exaggeration came from…

'I had backed into your corner and challenged you. I suspected that you were ready to take flight again and I cut short my time with the *notaire*,' Andreo volunteered, his hands dropping from her to accompany the speech.

At the stark look of reproach in his gaze, Pippa reddened with guilt. 'My thinking was all skewed and—you know? I was trying to save face too but I wasn't being fair to either of us in running away from things just because I couldn't handle them—'

'You need me to keep on proving myself to you. That's all and for what it's worth, I would have chased after you again, *carissima*,' Andreo confided huskily.

'And I would have done it again…and again until I won your trust.'

'Is that what I was doing?' That was when Pippa saw her own behaviour in a different light. On a subconscious level, she had been testing him out, hoping that he would make the effort to follow her and convince her that he was a guy she could rely on. 'Well, it won't be happening again. I haven't been fair to you. Apart from that misunderstanding we had about Lili Richards, you had been very honest with me—'

'What I had with Lili was strictly casual. I should have called Lili and told her I'd met you but ditching her by phone would have been tacky. It would also have felt like overkill when Lili and I had agreed that we were free agents before she left. I also…' his strong jaw-line squared and he forged on grimly, 'I also think that I was reluctant at that point to accept how important you had become in my life, *cara*.'

He was firing that fantasy element in her imagination again. 'Important? Was I?'

Andreo frowned. 'I haven't been serious about a woman since Fia.'

'My goodness…you don't get serious much.' Pippa heard herself make that inane comment in a distinctly squeaky voice.

'I made such an ass of myself over her that I had no wish to allow any woman that much power over me again,' Andreo confided with a grimace.

Pippa smoothed her hand in a soothing gesture across one broad shoulder and her fingers lingered to maintain a physical connection between them. 'You were very young. You shouldn't be so hard on yourself.'

'I lost face in my own eyes. My family were very forgiving but I was deeply ashamed of my own lack of judgement,' Andreo admitted curtly. 'I fell in love with an imaginary image of Fia rather than with the woman she really was—'

'I made the same mistake with that student Pete when I was seventeen,' Pippa rushed to tell him. 'I saw him as Mr Perfect but I haven't done that with you...'

Andreo tensed and gazed down at her with rather touching wariness.

'I mean, I know you're not perfect! No human being is perfect,' Pippa hurried to add, recognising too late that he really, really wanted her to think he was the most perfect guy imaginable. 'But I swear you're the closest thing ever—'

'No...I've made too many mistakes. If anything had happened to you or to our baby today, I would never have forgiven myself for not telling you how I feel about you,' Andreo proclaimed.

'I felt the same way,' Pippa whispered tenderly.

'I've been a lost cause from the first night I saw you, *cara*,' Andreo interposed. 'Why do you think I was so hot for you? I've never felt anything that powerful before.'

Cheeks burning, and suspecting that he was referring to lust alone, Pippa mumbled, 'I hadn't either—'

Andreo looked down at her with glittering golden eyes and, closing his hands round hers in a sudden movement, breathed, 'Being with you feels wonderful but at the beginning that unnerved me—'

'Feeling wonderful unnerved you?'

His hands tightened on hers and she flinched, soon appreciating that he was so deep in serious thought that he had not a clue that he was crushing her fingers. 'Falling in love when you're not expecting it can be...'

Andreo hesitated in search of the right word '...traumatic.'

'Traumatic?' Pippa parroted as he released her hands to execute a restive movement towards the window.

Andreo swung back to her again. 'You didn't feel the same way...of course it was traumatic!' he pointed out. 'You were about one degree warmer than a freezer the next day, and the minute you found out who I was you wanted nothing to do with me!'

'But I did...I did feel the same way.' Her thoughts had only slowly reached the awareness that he had to be talking about having fallen for her. Pippa blinked rapidly. Andreo *loved* her? He loved her?

'Are you saying that you love me?' Andreo shot at her incredulously.

'To death...love you just so much,' she stressed, suffering from emotional overload and very near to tears in her over-excitement.

Andreo focused on her with dazed dark golden eyes. 'But you were leaving me again...'

Pippa nodded and compressed tremulous lips.

'For the *second* time,' Andreo emphasised.

Pippa nodded again, tears of regret clogging up her vocal cords.

'Even though I'd asked you to marry me...'

The tears overflowed and streamed in a silent river down her cheeks.

'But all that is *absolutely* OK!' Andreo insisted in panic at the sight of those tears. 'Honestly, I have no idea why I'm so full of complaints. I'm crazy about you and I'll be crazy about our baby too. I can forgive you for anything. Please don't cry, *amore*.'

'I can't help it...my emotions are all over the place and you only have to touch my heart a little at the minute and I could flood the sea with tears. I think it's my hormones, something to do with being pregnant.' Pippa loosed an embarrassed laugh. 'But I'm just so happy!'

Andreo caught her to him with two possessive hands and claimed her ripe mouth with hungry, demanding urgency and it was the best cure for tears imaginable.

'Happy...happy...happy,' she repeated, wicked, wanton excitement sending tiny little shivers through her as she stayed melded to his lean, powerful frame.

'And I think you need to lie down,' Andreo informed her huskily, vibrant amusement lighting his keen appraisal as he swept her up into his arms and began to mount the stairs to the master bedroom. 'I know *I* do...'

Pippa felt incredibly warm and safe: he loved her. All her fears had been empty fears born of her insecurity.

'Am I allowed to ask what changed your mind about babies?' Andreo prompted, lowering her down onto the bed with immense care.

'I think I was most scared of the responsibility. My parents had a bad marriage and my childhood suffered because of it,' Pippa confided awkwardly. 'I was afraid that if I had a child I would make him or her unhappy too.'

'I can understand that, *amore*. But if you valued yourself as I do, you would already know that you are far too sensitive to behave as your parents did.'

At that vote of confidence, her discomfiture melted. 'I felt different once I knew I was pregnant,' she admitted softly. 'I realised the baby would be part of both of us and all of a sudden our baby was this fascinating little person in his own right. I still worried about how I would measure up as a parent but I felt excited too.'

'You're such a perfectionist and so hard on yourself. I promise that I will never let you down,' Andreo swore with tender force. 'I was too impatient with you. In time, you will learn to trust me.'

'I trust you now but I'll still watch you like a hawk,' Pippa warned him cheerfully. 'There are desperate women out there.'

An appreciative grin slanted his wide, sensual mouth. 'Will you marry me now?'

'I'll think it over,' she dared, confident enough to tease him while still marvelling that he could have fallen in love with someone as ordinary as she believed herself to be.

Halfway out of his shirt, a virile wedge of bronzed muscular chest revealed, Andreo froze and groaned, 'If you want me in your bed again, you *have* to marry me.'

With a sense of joy and freedom entirely new to her, Pippa burst out laughing and feasted her eyes on his lean, darkly handsome features. 'If I agree to marry you as soon as it can be arranged, can I have something on account?'

All male provocation at that request, Andreo let his shirt drop to the floor with a flourish. 'So you want to marry me?'

Pippa arched her toes so that her sandals fell off and heaved a blissful sigh of agreement. 'Definitely...do you mind if I ask you how *much* you love me?' she muttered more shyly.

Andreo rested adoring eyes on her. 'Head over heels and crazy about you. Enough to last two lifetimes at least, *amore*.'

Reassured, Pippa stretched up her arms and linked them round him to draw him down to her, all the while maintaining her loving connection with his appreciative gaze. 'I love you every bit as much...'

* * *

Four weeks later, Pippa married her Italian boss.

The run-up to the wedding was an incredibly busy time
for her. She spent almost two weeks flitting about Italy
getting to know Andreo's family: his fashionable and
friendly mother, Giulietta, his six-foot-two-inch teenage
brother, Marco, and his three older sisters and their re-
spective husbands and children. The D'Alessio clan made
an enormous fuss of Pippa and she went from feeling
rather intimidated by the sheer number of Andreo's gre-
garious relatives to feeling warmed by their affectionate
acceptance of her as Andreo's chosen bride.

Giulietta D'Alessio persuaded Pippa to allow her to
organise the wedding and having little taste for that kind
of thing, Pippa was delighted to hand over the responsibility for what was already promising to be a major
social event.

Andreo and Pippa were married in Rome. Tabby and
Hilary had gone shopping with Pippa to help her choose
her wedding outfit. She selected a sleeveless bodice made
of duchess satin and a long swirling skirt of Thai silk
and a detachable embroidered train. Wearing it on the
day with the superb diamond tiara that was a gift from
her bridegroom and a short delicate veil, she was much
admired as a stunningly elegant bride.

Tabby acted as matron of honour and Hilary was to be
a bridesmaid but had to surrender the honour to Andreo's
eldest niece a week before the ceremony when her little
sister, Emma, was rushed into hospital for emergency
surgery. Andreo's boyhood friend, Sal Rissone, was best
man. In his speech the best man confessed that he had
first suspected that Andreo was in love the minute he'd
begun clock-watching at the office and seeking privacy
to make his phone calls.

'You look so beautiful you take my breath away, *bella*

mia,' Andreo told his bride when they finally got a moment alone together on the dance floor at their reception.

Pippa's heart had not stopped racing since she'd seen Andreo waiting for her at the altar. As befitted the occasion, his lean, dark, devastating features were serious but his proud, possessive gaze had remained welded to her with intoxicating intensity. Over the past frantic month, Andreo's need to catch up with work and clear the space in his busy schedule for a honeymoon had ensured that they had had little time together. When he drew her close, she shivered at the contact with his lean, powerful body, ultra sensitive to his raw, virile masculinity and the wicked promise of the sensual smile curving his beautiful mouth.

'I want to be alone with you so badly I *ache*,' Andreo admitted with such feeling force that she blushed to the roots of her hair and struggled to damp down her own wanton response to his unashamed hunger for her.

Only a minute later, Marco cut in on Andreo to dance with her. His youthful features held all the promise of the same good looks that distinguished her bridegroom. Having cheerfully ignored his older brother's protests, he sighed with mock reproach, 'It's not cool to cling to each other the way you two do.'

Pippa laughed. 'We don't,' she said and angled her head round to try and spot where Andreo had gone.

'Don't worry…he hasn't gone far.' It was Marco's turn to laugh for his older brother was poised on the edge of the floor, his attention exclusively pinned to his beautiful bride. 'I can see I'm going to get a lot of mileage out of teasing you.'

For their honeymoon, Andreo took Pippa to his birthplace on the island of Ischia in the Gulf of Naples. There she was carried over the threshold of the magnificent villa that Andreo regarded as his home. He and his siblings had been born on Ischia but his widowed mother had moved her family to Rome after her husband's death.

After breakfast the next morning, Pippa walked out of their bedroom onto the sun-drenched marble terrace. She was enchanted by the glorious views. The chalk white houses were set against a landscape of old stone walls, silvery olive groves and lush green vineyards and backed by the deep sparkling blue of the sea.

'So this is where we're going to live,' she murmured, resting back against Andreo with the perfect trust of a woman who knew she was loved. 'Have you always spent most of your time here?'

Andreo closed gentle arms round her and spread lean fingers in a tender speaking gesture across the faint protuberance of her tummy. 'No, but now that I'm to become a father I shall need to cut down on my trips abroad, *cara*. Off the tourist track, the pace of life is slower here. It's a wonderful place to raise a child.'

Contentment filled Pippa to overflowing. Turning within his embrace, she gazed up into his darkly handsome features with her heart in her eyes, but there was still one tiny nagging concern to be faced. Breathing in deep, she worried at her lower lip before saying shyly, 'I'm probably being very silly, but are you going to end up getting bored with me?'

'*Dio mio!* What are you talking about?' Andreo demanded in frowning disconcertion. 'I could never become bored with you or what we have together. It is more than I ever hoped to have with any woman—'

'Even though I'll never be in the diamond-studded handcuffs line?' Pippa prompted in an effort to be more specific about what he might or might not miss in the future.

Andreo tensed and wondered which he was going to put first: his rampant reputation as a living legend in the bedroom or his bride's peace of mind? The only diamond-studded handcuffs he had ever purchased had been of the miniaturised variety, quite literally a gold charm for a bracelet, the most casual of gifts. A kiss-and-tell story sold by the same lady who had briefly shared his bed had first employed the outrageous lie presumably to make her revelations seem more newsworthy.

'All that's behind me…' But as he looked down into Pippa's anxious blue eyes Andreo's conscience stirred and he released his breath in a sudden hiss. He confessed the truth about the diamond-studded handcuffs.

Pippa looked up at him for a long, timeless moment and then she just crumpled into helpless giggles. Every time she tried to stop laughing, she would recall the rueful look on his face as he chose to make that lowering admission and it would set her off into whoops again.

'But now that I've found the woman of my dreams, I can at last live out my every sexual fantasy,' Andreo drawled in a super-fast recovery, bending down and scooping her up to carry her back into the bedroom.

Hot-cheeked, eyes startled, Pippa gazed up at him. 'Are you serious?'

He came down on the bed with her and covered her soft pink mouth with the passionate demand of his. Erotic heat sizzled along her every nerve ending and she quivered.

'How serious would you like me to be, *amore*?' Andreo teased and then he told her all over again how much he loved her and she smiled, buoyant with joy and trust.

Seven months later, Pippa gave birth to their first child. She enjoyed an easy pregnancy and delivery. They called their infant daughter Lucia. She was an exceptionally pretty baby with her father's eyes and her mother's cinnamon curls and both her parents were besotted with her.

They took Lucia to France with them when they attended the christening of Tabby and Christien's second son, Fabien. The two couples had become fast friends and distance did not get in the way of their socialising. Andreo even asked Tabby to paint a miniature portrait of Lucia to mark the occasion of the first anniversary of his marriage.

The week in which their wedding anniversary fell, Andreo and Pippa left their beloved daughter in the care of her grandmother, Giulietta, and went to stay at the idyllic priory in the Dordogne, which held a special place in both their hearts.

'Would you marry me again if you had a choice?' Pippa asked daringly the night they arrived.

'Faster than the speed of the light, *bella mia*. I love you and I love having you and Lucia in my life,' Andreo intoned huskily.

Pippa looked up into his stunning golden eyes and linked both arms round him tight. 'I love you too,' she whispered, her heartbeat racing as he claimed her mouth with his.

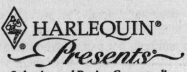

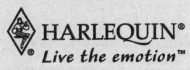

If you enjoyed what you just read,
then we've got an offer you can't resist!

Take 2 bestselling love stories FREE!
Plus get a FREE surprise gift!

Clip this page and mail it to Harlequin Reader Service®

IN U.S.A.	IN CANADA
3010 Walden Ave.	P.O. Box 609
P.O. Box 1867	Fort Erie, Ontario
Buffalo, N.Y. 14240-1867	L2A 5X3

YES! Please send me 2 free Harlequin Presents® novels and my free surprise gift. After receiving them, if I don't wish to receive anymore, I can return the shipping statement marked cancel. If I don't cancel, I will receive 6 brand-new novels every month, before they're available in stores! In the U.S.A., bill me at the bargain price of $3.57 plus 25¢ shipping & handling per book and applicable sales tax, if any*. In Canada, bill me at the bargain price of $4.24 plus 25¢ shipping & handling per book and applicable taxes**. That's the complete price and a savings of at least 10% off the cover prices—what a great deal! I understand that accepting the 2 free books and gift places me under no obligation ever to buy any books. I can always return a shipment and cancel at any time. Even if I never buy another book from Harlequin, the 2 free books and gift are mine to keep forever.

106 HDN DNTZ
306 HDN DNT2

Name	(PLEASE PRINT)	
Address	Apt.#	
City	State/Prov.	Zip/Postal Code

* Terms and prices subject to change without notice. Sales tax applicable in N.Y.
** Canadian residents will be charged applicable provincial taxes and GST.

All orders subject to approval. Offer limited to one per household and not valid to current Harlequin Presents® subscribers.

® are registered trademarks of Harlequin Enterprises Limited.

PRES02   ©2001 Harlequin Enterprises Limited

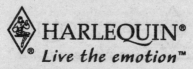

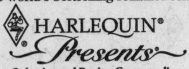

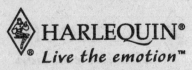